THE STEEL SPRING

Born in 1926, Per Wahlöö was a Swedish writer
and journalist who, alongside his own novels,
collaborated with his wife, Maj Sjöwall, on the
bestselling Martin Beck crime series which are
credited as inspiring writers as varied as Agatha
Christie, Henning Mankell and Jonathan Franzen.
In 1971 the fourth novel in the series, *The
Laughing Policeman*, won an Edgar Award from
the Mystery Writers of America. Per Wahlöö died
in 1975.

Sarah Death has translated the work of many
Swedish authors from the nineteenth to the
twenty-first century, including Alexander
Ahndoril, Steve Sem-Sandberg and Carl-Johan
Vallgren, and Norwegian Linn Ullman (*A
Blessed Child* was named Translated Novel of
the Year by the *Independent*). She has twice
won the triennial George Bernard Shaw Prize,
for Kerstin Ekman's *The Angel House*, and Ellen
Mattson's *Snow*. In 2008 she was awarded the
Swedish Academy's Translation Prize.

PER WAHLÖÖ

The Steel Spring

TRANSLATED FROM THE SWEDISH BY
Sarah Death

VINTAGE BOOKS
London

Published by Vintage 2011

2 4 6 8 10 9 7 5 3 1

Copyright © Per Wahlöö 1968
English translation copyright © Sarah Death 2012

Per Wahlöö has asserted his right under the Copyright, Designs and Patents Act 1988 to be
identified as the author of this work.

First published in Sweden by P.A.Norstedt & Söners Förlag
under the title *Stålspånget*

First published in Great Britain in 1970 by
Michael Joseph

Vintage
Random House, 20 Vauxhall Bridge Road,
London SW1V 2SA

www.vintage-books.co.uk

Addresses for companies within The Random House Group Limited
can be found at: www.randomhouse.co.uk/offices.htm

The Random House Group Limited Reg. No. 954009

A CIP catalogue record for this book
is available from the British Library

ISBN 9780099554752

The Random House Group Limited supports The Forest Stewardship Council (FSC®), the
leading international forest certification organisation. Our books carrying the FSC label
are printed on FSC® certified paper. FSC is the only forest certification scheme endorsed
by the leading environmental organisations, including Greenpeace. Our paper procurement
policy can be found at www.randomhouse.co.uk/environment

Typeset in Minion by Palimpsest Book Production Limited
Falkirk, Stirlingshire

Printed and bound in Great Britain by
CPI Group (UK) Ltd, Croydon, CR0 4YY

For Maj

CHAPTER 1

Jensen received the letter in the morning post.

He had risen early and packed his suitcase, and when the letterbox rattled he was already in the hall with his hat and overcoat on. He bent down to pick up the letter. As he straightened his back, pain shot through the right side of his diaphragm, as if a high-speed boring tool was rotating in his guts. He was so used to the pain that he scarcely registered it.

He put the letter in his pocket without looking at it, picked up his case, went down to the car and drove to work.

At one minute to nine he turned in through the archway to the Sixteenth District police station and parked in the yellow-painted rectangle marked INSPECTOR. He got out, retrieved his case from the boot and scanned the yard. Outside the entrance to the arrest suite there was a white ambulance with red crosses on the doors, which were open at the back. Two young men in white boiler suits, their faces indifferent, were nonchalantly and carelessly shoving in a stretcher. A few metres from them, a police constable in a green uniform was hosing a pool of blood from the tarmac. The woman on the stretcher was young and blonde and had a bloodstained bandage round her neck. Jensen glanced at her and turned to the man with the hose.

'Dead?'

The police constable pinched the hose to cut off the flow of water and attempted to come to attention.

'Yes, Inspector.'

Jensen said no more, but turned and went into the reception area, nodded to the policeman behind the wooden counter and walked over to the spiral stairs.

His office on the floor above was stuffy and stale smelling, and the radiator under the window was clanking and hissing. The police station was housed in one of the oldest buildings in a part of the city that otherwise consisted of nothing but steel, glass and concrete. The arrest suite had been extended and rebuilt a few years before, but the rest of the building had never been modernised, and soon the whole lot was to be pulled down to make way for a new bypass. As soon as the new central detoxification unit was ready, the district would be taken out of use. The prospect did not bother Jensen.

He hung up his outdoor things, opened the window a little way and sat down at his desk. He read through the report from the previous night and corrected it minutely in ballpoint pen before putting his signature in the margin. He fished in his inside pocket, took out the letter and looked at it.

Jensen was a man of normal build and ordinary appearance with short grey hair and an impassive expression. He was fifty and had served twenty-nine years in the Sixteenth District.

He was still studying the letter when the door opened and the police doctor came in.

'You should knock,' said Jensen.

'Sorry. I didn't know you were coming in today.' Jensen looked at the clock.

'My replacement doesn't take over until ten,' he said. 'What sort of night has it been?'

'Normal. We had a sudden death this morning. A woman. The report hasn't been written yet.'

2

Jensen nodded.

'Not in the cell,' said the doctor. 'In the yard. She cut her throat as soon as the arrest officer let her out. With a bit of mirror she had in her handbag.'

'Careless,' said Jensen.

'We can't take everything off them.'

'Can't we?'

'Anyway, she'd already sobered up and had her injection. And the officers who did the body search didn't think it was glass. Glass pocket mirrors are supposed to be banned.'

'They're not banned,' said Jensen. 'They don't make them any more.'

The police doctor was a tall, relatively young man with spiky red hair and angular features. He knew his job and was the best doctor the district had had in the last ten years. Jensen had a lot of time for him.

'I'm beginning to question the method,' said the red-haired doctor with a shake of his head.

'What method?'

'Blending the alcohol with that muck. The stuff that's meant to wean them off it. Admittedly the rate of arrests for drinking hasn't gone up these past two years, but . . .'

Jensen regarded him stonily.

'But what?'

'But on the other hand, the suicide rate's on the up. The depression cases are getting worse.'

'The statistics contradict what you're saying.'

'You know as well as I do how much the official statistics are worth. Take a look at your own confidential reports on accidents and cases of sudden death. Like the woman this morning. We can't just gloss over it and pretend nothing's happening.'

3

He thrust his hands in the pockets of his white coat and looked out of the window.

'Have you heard the latest? They're thinking of putting pain-killers and fluoride in the drinking water. It's medical madness.'

'You ought to watch your tongue.'

'Quite possibly,' the doctor said drily.

There was silence in the room. Jensen scrutinised the letter he had received in the morning post. The envelope was white and it had been addressed by a machine. Inside were a white printed card and a steel-blue, gummed stamp with perforated edges and a picture of a bridge spanning a deep ravine, with a single word in the middle: YES. Jensen opened the middle drawer of his desk, took out a wooden ruler and measured the card. The doctor, watching him attentively, said:

'Why are you measuring it?'

'I don't know,' said Jensen.

He put the ruler back and shut the drawer.

'Old one, that. Wooden. Steel-edged.'

'Yes,' said Jensen. 'I've had it twenty-nine years. Ever since I came here. They don't make them any more.'

The card measured fourteen centimetres by ten. On the front there was a printed address; on the back there was a series of dashes in a rectangle, to show where the stamp was to go. Above it was some text.

Do you believe in the policies of the Accord? Are you ready to play an active part in the battle against the enemies of the country, inside and outside? Affix the sticker as indicated. Do not forget to add your signature. NB. This card is not to be franked.

Below the rectangle there was a dotted line where the sender was to sign his or her name. Jensen turned the card over and looked at the address.

Central Statistical Office, Ministry of the Interior. Box 1000.

'Some kind of opinion poll,' said the doctor with a shrug. 'Everybody seems to have had one of those cards. Except me.'

Jensen said nothing.

'Or perhaps some kind of loyalty test. In the run-up to the election.'

'The election,' said Jensen.

'Yes, in a month's time. If that's what it is, then it's pretty bloody superfluous. Waste of state resources.'

Jensen pulled the desk drawer open again and took out a sponge pad of green rubber, marked POLICE PROPERTY. He felt it with his fingertips. It was dry, and he got to his feet and left the room. Went to the toilet and moistened the sponge under the washbasin tap.

Jensen returned to his office, sat down at his desk, ran the blue sticker over the sponge pad and placed it with pedantic care in the rectangular space. Then he put the card in the metal tray for outgoing post and replaced the sponge in his desk drawer. Closed the drawer. The doctor observed him with a faint smile and said:

'Your office equipment looks as if it belongs in a museum.'

Then he glanced from the wall clock to the packed suitcase over by the door.

'Ah well, two hours from now you'll be on the plane.'

'Will I die?' said Inspector Jensen.

The doctor shot him an enquiring look. He paused, and then said:

'Very probably.'

CHAPTER 2

'Naturally you're in with a chance,' said the doctor. 'Otherwise neither I nor any other responsible person would have suggested the trip. They know their stuff over there.'

Jensen nodded.

'You ought to have had the problem seen to several years ago, of course. Are you in a lot of pain?'

'Yes.'

'Now, as well?'

'Yes.'

'On the other hand, there wasn't much they could have done for you several years ago. The operation technique is still at an experimental stage. In this country they've barely got round to thinking about it. And you're in a pretty bad state.'

Jensen nodded.

'But as I say, you're in with a chance.'

'What sort of chance?'

'Impossible to say. Maybe ten per cent, maybe only five. In all probability even less than that.'

Jensen nodded.

'Bear in mind that in the space of less than five seconds, all the blood in the body sluices through the liver. The liver is the great factory of the body. Can it really be transplanted? I don't know.'

'We'll know in a few days' time.'

'Yes,' said the doctor.

He looked at Jensen contemplatively.

'Would you like something for the pain?'

'No.'

'It's a long journey.'

'Yes.'

'Have you got a return ticket?'

'No.'

'Very encouraging,' the doctor said sarcastically.

He lapsed into silence and appeared in doubt about something. In the end Jensen said:

'What is it?'

'Something I've been meaning to ask you for a long time.'

'What?'

'They say you've never failed to solve a case. Is that true?'

'Yes, that's right,' said Inspector Jensen.

The telephone rang.

'Sixteenth District police. Inspector here.'

'Jensen?'

Jensen had not heard the police chief's voice for four years, still less seen him. Was he ringing to say goodbye?

'Yes.'

'Excellent. You'll be receiving written orders within the next few minutes. They must be carried out with all possible speed.'

'Understood.'

'Good.'

Jensen looked at the electric clock on the wall.

'I go on sick leave in eighteen minutes' time,' he said.

'Oh? Are you ill?'

'Yes.'

PER WAHLÖÖ

'Sorry to hear that, Jensen. You'll have to brief your stand-in.'

'Yes.'

'It's a matter of extreme importance. Orders from . . . well, the highest authority.'

'Understood.'

The police chief paused. Finally he said:

'Good luck then, Jensen.'

'Thank you.'

Inspector Jensen replaced the receiver. The police chief had sounded nervous and harassed. Perhaps he always sounded like that.

'In the space of less than five seconds,' said the doctor. 'All the blood in your body.'

Jensen nodded. A few moments later he said:

'Where are they transferring you to when this district closes down?'

'The central detoxification unit, I assume. And you?'

The doctor suddenly stopped himself. Changed the subject slightly.

'Have you seen the detoxification unit?' he said.

Jensen shook his head.

'It's vast. Looks like a gigantic prison. The biggest complex I've ever seen. And what about you?'

Jensen said nothing.

'Sorry,' said the doctor.

'Don't worry about it,' said Jensen.

There was a knock at the door. A police officer in a green uniform came in, stood to attention and handed over a red file. Jensen signed for it and the constable left the room.

'Red,' said the doctor. 'Everything's top secret these days.'

9

He put his head to one side so he could read the operational code name.

'What does that mean? Steel Spring?'

'Don't know,' said Jensen. 'Steel Spring. I've never seen the name before.' He broke the seal and took out the orders. They consisted of a single typewritten sheet.

'What's that?'

'An arrest list.'

'Really?' the doctor said dubiously. 'But nobody commits crimes in this country, do they?'

Jensen read the text slowly through.

'Nobody commits crimes and nobody gives birth. Everybody thinks the same. Nobody's happy and nobody's unhappy. Except the ones who kill themselves.' The doctor stopped and smiled a quick, melancholy smile.

'You're right,' he said. 'I really ought to mind my tongue.'

'You're impulsive.'

'Yes. Anything interesting in your arrest list?'

'In a way,' said Inspector Jensen. 'Your name's on it.'

'That's good. There's research showing how important it is before a major operation for the patient to joke and display a sense of humour. It shows zest for life. Right, I must be off now. And so must you. You don't want to miss the plane. Best of luck.'

'Thanks,' said Inspector Jensen.

The instant the door closed, he picked up the telephone, dialled three digits and said:

'Jensen here. The doctor is just on his way down to reception. Arrest him and put him in preventive detention.'

'The police doctor?'

'Yes. And be quick about it.'

He ended the call and immediately rang another three-digit number.

'Jensen here. Ask the head of the plainclothes patrol to come up. And ring for a taxi.'

The electric wall clock was showing one minute to ten as the head of the plainclothes patrol came into the room.

'I'm on sick leave from ten o'clock,' said Jensen. 'As you know, you're to take over until further notice.'

'Thank you, Inspector.'

'Don't thank me. As you know, I've never had a particularly high opinion of you, and you didn't get the post on my recommendation.'

The man opened his mouth to say something but apparently changed his mind.

'Here's a list of forty-three individuals who live or are active in the district. They are to be apprehended immediately, searched and put into preventive custody. The regional prosecutor's office will send officers over to fetch them later today.'

'Er, Inspector?'

'Yes, what is it?'

'What have these people done?'

'I don't know.' Jensen glanced at the clock. 'And anyway, you're the inspector now. The car's in the usual space. The keys are in the pen tray.'

He stood up and put on his hat and overcoat. The man at the desk studied the arrest list and said:

'But they're all . . .'

He broke off.

'That's right,' said Jensen. 'They're all doctors. Goodbye.'

He picked up his suitcase and went.

CHAPTER 3

The airport lay to the south, a long way from the city. Getting there by car from the Sixteenth District police station took an hour and a half if you were lucky. The journey had been considerably longer in the past, but in recent years the inner city had turned increasingly into one huge traffic-flow system, an apparent jumble of flyovers and criss-crossing motorways. Virtually all the older buildings had been pulled down to make more living space for automobiles, a planning solution that had resulted in a city centre apparently consisting of soaring columns of glass, steel and concrete. Divided up into squares and corralled by the multi-lane highways were groups of multi-storey car parks, office buildings and department stores with small shops, cinemas, petrol stations and gleaming chrome snack bars on the ground floors. Many years earlier, when this city plan was being implemented, critical voices had been raised to say that the system would make the city inhuman and uninhabitable. The experts had brushed off the criticism. They argued that a modern city should be built not for pedestrians and horse-drawn carriages but for cars. As on so many other issues, both sides had subsequently been proved right. This was entirely in the spirit of the Accord.

The taxi moved swiftly through the inner city, plunged into the road tunnel by the Ministry of the Interior and surfaced in an industrial area eight kilometres further south.

It continued over a bridge and approached the suburban belt.

The air was chilly and the skies were cloudless on this early autumn day. Hoar frost veiled the concrete surface of the motorway, and the greyish air, poisoned with exhaust fumes, lay like an enormous bell over people, cars, roads and built-up areas. The experts at the Ministry for Public Health calculated that the polluted air now extended fifty or sixty metres into the air. Just a few years before, the bell of air had been estimated to be just fifteen metres high, with a diameter of twelve kilometres. The latest measurements at ground level showed the area had more than doubled. The investigation had been carried out as part of a routine programme, and had not caused any measures to be taken. The report had been declared confidential, since it was feared that the findings could cause anxiety to certain parts of the population, but before that it had been circulated among senior police officers. Jensen had read it and passed on the papers without comment.

The traffic was dense but fast moving. The sides of the road were lined with coloured posters reminding people of the forthcoming democratic elections. Posters bearing the image of a lantern-jawed man with thinning hair and vivid blue eyes alternated with others that were just a letter of the alphabet, a big pink 'A'. The man was the future head of the government, an individual considered to represent the totally interdependent concepts of welfare, security and accord better than anyone else. Married into the royal family, he had previously been the head of the National Confederation. He was currently the Minister for the Interior. Before the grand coalition he had been a social democrat.

The taxi driver put on the brakes as a policeman signalled

to him to stop. They were on their way up on to a long bridge, and ahead of them, constables in green uniforms were busy with a traffic jam. The driver wound down the side window, took a white handkerchief out of his breast pocket and blew his nose. He looked impassively at the grey-black marks on the handkerchief, cleared his throat and spat out of the window.

'Another demonstration,' he said. 'We'll be through in no time.'

Thirty seconds later, the police constable waved the traffic ahead, and the driver engaged gear and eased the car forward.

'Morons,' he said. 'Taking up a whole lane.'

They met the march up on the bridge. It was not a particularly large one. Jensen made a practised assessment of its size and composition. Between two thousand, five hundred and three thousand people, divided roughly equally between the sexes, and a surprising number of children for a country with a birth rate in permanent decline. Some of the children were so small that they were in pushchairs or sitting on their parents' shoulders. The demonstrators were carrying placards and banners, and Jensen read the slogans as the march went past. Some were easy to understand. They complained about issues like poor air quality and non-recyclable packaging, but also about the current government. 'Accorded to Death' was a recurring slogan. But most of the texts were incomprehensible. They were about solidarity with other races and foreign peoples, countries he'd never heard of and combinations of letters he didn't understand, but assumed to be acronyms. Some of the marchers were carrying pictures of foreigners with strange names, presumably heads of state or political leaders. The intention appeared to be to sing the praises of some of these and denounce others. There were also placards with a variety of old-fashioned

and obsolete slogans and sentiments like class struggle, prole-
tariat, capitalism, imperialism, the working masses, and world
revolution. At the front and back of the march there were massed
red flags.

The people in the cars and along the sides of the road seemed
wholly unaffected, doing no more than glance distractedly at
the flags and placards. The onlookers seemed simply indifferent.
Admittedly they all appeared dissatisfied and nervous, with
nowhere to go, but their reaction had nothing to do with the
demonstration. Jensen knew this from experience.

The demonstrators were marching four abreast. The police
calmly and systematically made way for them and kept the
traffic moving. There was no commotion; the whole thing
seemed harmless.

The procession had passed by, and the taxi driver accelerated
and asked without much interest:

'Who are that lot? Some kind of socialists?'

'I don't know.'

The driver looked at his watch.

'Well they're holding up the traffic. We lost at least three or
four minutes back there on the bridge. Why don't the police
clear them off the streets?'

Jensen said nothing. He knew the answer to the question,
nevertheless.

Demonstrations of that kind had been going on for the
previous four years. They were still relatively insignificant in
scale, but were being staged increasingly often, with participant
numbers seeming to swell each time. The marches always
followed roughly the same pattern. They began somewhere in
the suburbs and headed for the city centre, either to some
foreign embassy or to the coalition parties' central offices, where

the march would break up of its own volition once the partici-
pants had chanted slogans for half an hour or so. There was
no legislation outlawing demonstrations. In theory it was for
the police themselves to decide on an appropriate response. In
practice, things worked rather differently. The Ministry of the
Interior initially gave orders that the demonstrations were to
be halted and dispersed, that placards and banners were to be
examined, and confiscated if any of the slogans were considered
indecent, distressing or offensive. The clearly stated aim was
to protect the general public from experiences that might put
people on edge or spread a sense of insecurity. But police
intervention had exactly the opposite effect. Despite the fact
that these were not mass demonstrations but generally just
groups of a few hundred people, attempts to break up the
demonstrations led to skirmishes, disorder and serious disruption of the traffic. After a time, the police were ordered to use
other methods, but there were no specific instructions on the
measures to be taken. The forces of law and order did their
best. They stopped some marches, for example, while they
subjected all those taking part to breath tests. The constant rise
in drunkenness had led the government some years previously
to pass a law making the abuse of alcohol illegal, not only in
public places but also in the home. Being under the influence
of alcohol in any setting at all had therefore become a criminal
offence, a fact that had increased the burden of police work
almost to breaking point. The new legislation had had no
impact on drinking to excess, and it soon proved ineffective in
clamping down on the demonstrations as well, since the
marchers were never under the influence of alcohol. This
strange circumstance was to Jensen's mind the only essential
feature that distinguished the demonstrators from the

population as a whole. Two years before, the alcohol policy had changed, with the new focus on price rises and chemical substances. In the meantime, the police had been ordered to leave the demonstrators in peace. It was decided by the government that the police should confine themselves to keeping certain foreign embassies under surveillance and directing the traffic along the march routes. Since then, the demonstrations had passed off calmly, but they were happening increasingly often, and more and more people were joining in, even though there was never a word about them in the papers, on radio or on television. There were rumours, however, of some anxiety at government level. In the most recent elections, voter turnout had slumped in a very disquieting way. No one understood why. Only vague figures had been released for publication, and these were commented on only in the most general terms. And the collaborating parties were engaging this year in propaganda more concentrated than they had ever employed before. The campaign had been launched back in the late spring, and was now accelerating to its peak.

Jensen had no clear conception of what the real aim of the demonstrations might be, but he thought he had some idea of how and when they had started.

The pain was intense and caught him off guard; it seared through the right side of his diaphragm, wild and merciless. Everything went black, he hunched over and clenched his teeth so as not to whimper like a dog about to be whipped.

The driver squinted at him suspiciously but said nothing.

It seemed a very long time until the spasm ebbed away and the pain reverted to the usual dull ache. In actual fact it was only a matter of minutes. He was panting for breath; he gasped for air and managed to suppress a fit of coughing.

When he looked up again, they were just passing the suburb where his own apartment lay. The taxi was keeping up a decent speed on the motorway.

'We'll be there in half an hour,' said the driver.

The suburb where Inspector Jensen lived consisted of thirty-six eight-storey blocks of flats, set out in four parallel lines. Between the rows of blocks there were car parks, grassy areas, and play pavilions of transparent plastic for what few children there were. It was all very neatly laid out.

Further south, the tower blocks grew more spectral and decayed. It was some years since the authorities had solved the housing shortage with a building programme that produced endless blocks of flats like the one where he lived himself. So-called uniform estates, with standard apartments, all identical. But even back then, the older of the tower blocks, paradoxically often located long distances from the inner city, began to lose their occupants. They were abandoned by shopkeepers, property owners, the authorities and the tenants, in that order. Falling birth rates and the shrinking population naturally played their part, too. Deprived of communications and any way of supporting themselves – in the end they also had their water and electricity supplies turned off – the suburbs in question very quickly degenerated into slums. Most of the blocks of flats had only come into existence because private developers hoped to make a quick profit from the housing shortage. They were poorly built, and many of them had already collapsed, sinking like sinister grave mounds into the scrubby undergrowth. The experts at the Ministry of Social Affairs had promoted the concept of letting these residential areas gradually empty themselves and ultimately collapse. Such suburbs were called 'self-clearance areas' and were to be viewed as naturally occurring rubbish dumps. The experts' projections had proved valid except on one point. About five per cent of the flats in the blocks that were still standing continued to be occupied by people that the society of the Accord had somehow failed to take care of. People were sometimes even killed when the old blocks of flats collapsed, as they often did, but neither the property owners nor the authorities were held legally responsible in such cases. A blanket warning not to live in abandoned apartment blocks had been issued, and that was sufficient.

Jensen looked out of the side window. A self-clearance area stretched away to the right of the motorway. Roughly a third of the blocks were still standing. They were silhouetted like sooty pillars against the ice-blue autumn sky. In the distance he could see a few children playing amongst stacks of wrecked cars and piles of non-reusable glass bottles and indestructible plastic packaging.

His gaze was calm and expressionless.

Fifteen minutes later, the taxi stopped outside the airport terminal building. Inspector Jensen paid and climbed out.

He was still in a lot of pain.

CHAPTER 4

The room had two windows with thin, pale blue curtains. The walls were dark blue and the ceiling was white. The bed was also white. It was made of wood and ingeniously constructed.

Jensen lay perfectly still on his back, arms at his sides. If he moved his right hand five centimetres he could reach the button and ring the bell. If he did that, it would take no longer than fifteen seconds for the door to open and the nurse to come in. He didn't touch the button. The only thing he could think about was not being sure what the date was. It might be the first of November, but it could also be the second or even the third. He knew he had been in this room for about two months, but he didn't know exactly how long, and that irritated him.

He also knew he was alive. This did not surprise him beyond a vague sense of surprise at not being surprised.

By the far window stood a basket chair. For the past two weeks he had been allowed to sit in that chair twice a day, half an hour in the morning and half an hour in the afternoon. It was afternoon now. He was aware of something that might be a desire to sit in the chair by the window. It was many years since he had felt anything like that.

The door opened. The man who came in had on a pale grey suit and was of slim build and very tanned. He had dark brown eyes, black curly hair slicked back from his face, and a thin black moustache. He nodded to Jensen and stood at the foot of the bed. As he was flicking through the sheaf of notes hanging from the bedpost, he took out a yellowish cigarette with a long cardboard holder, put it between his lips and rolled it distractedly from one side of his mouth to the other before fishing out a box of matches and lighting up. Then he dropped the dead match on the floor and came gliding to the head of the bed, where he bent over Jensen and looked him in the eye.

Jensen felt he had had that face in front of him on countless occasions, at brief intervals, for as long as he could remember. The expression in the brown eyes had shifted; it had been worried, soothing, curious, resigned, enquiring or sad. The smell, on the other hand, had always remained the same: hair oil and tobacco smoke. Jensen had a vision of having once seen this man in a mask, with an orange rubber cap pulled well down over his black curls. That time, their surroundings had been drenched in a caustic, blue-white light and the man had been wearing something that looked like a butcher's apron. He knew with absolute certainty that the man had once, a very long time ago, shaken him by the hand and said something guttural and completely incomprehensible that presumably meant hello or welcome. Or perhaps he had simply been saying his name.

Today, the man looked cheerful. He smiled and nodded encouragingly, tapped his cigarette ash nonchalantly on to the floor, turned and left the room with rapid steps.

Soon after, the nurse appeared. She, too, was tanned and had dark, curly hair, but her eyes were grey. She was wearing blue canvas shoes and a short-sleeved white overall buttoned down the back. Her legs and arms were muscular and shapely. Like the doctor's, her movements were quick and supple and her touch was light. Jensen knew she was amazingly strong.

She had a permanent smile now, even when dealing with bedpans and urine bottles, but he had very often seen her grave and thoughtful, with compressed lips and her black eyebrows knitted in a frown.

She did not smoke or use any cosmetics, but she sometimes smelt of soap. Today he sensed only a vaguely astringent smell, which was presumably her own. It reminded him of something. When she had drawn back the bedclothes and tucked up his nightshirt, she washed him with a sponge. As she was bending over his legs, he observed the shape of her back and hips beneath the fabric. He wondered what she was wearing under the white overall. He could not remember ever having thought anything like that before.

The nurse had full lips and short black hairs on her shins. When she smiled you could see that her teeth were rather uneven but very white.

These two, the doctor and the nurse, had comprised his only direct contact with the world for a long time. He understood nothing of what they said, and by now they had stopped saying things, anyway. Once the doctor had had a newspaper with him, but it had no pictures and the letters of the alphabet were symbols he had never seen before.

The nurse had very suntanned hands and no rings on her fingers. Once when she thought he was asleep she had scratched herself between the legs.

When Jensen was sitting in the basket chair by the window, he could see out over a lawn with paved paths and little trees with pink or white flowers.

Men and women in blue gowns like the one he had on himself were strolling along the paths or sitting at small stone tables playing something, presumably chess. The grounds were not large, and beyond them ran a road where yellow trolleybuses rattled by. Once he had seen a camel out there.

On the other side of the road there was a factory. Every morning thousands of people, mainly women of different ages, would stream in through the gates. Many had small children with them. They left the children in a low, yellow-brick building to the right of the factory entrance. Some of the children whined and cried when their mothers left them, but within a few minutes they could be seen running around the playground outside the yellow building. They played and made plenty of noise. The women who looked after the children wore white cotton housecoats buttoned at the front. They all seemed to be expecting babies and he worked out that they were simply members of the workforce who had fallen pregnant and been automatically transferred to nursery duties.

There was laughter and a buzz of conversation in the morning when the women arrived for work in the factory and in the afternoon when they went home. Sometimes they would sing.

Jensen was not actually in pain any more, but he could not walk properly and felt very tired. He slept almost twenty hours a day.

One day the doctor appeared with a newspaper again, pointed to a headline and spoke quickly and agitatedly. When he realised Jensen did not understand a word, he shrugged and left.

The nurse was twenty-five at most. When they took their walks in the grounds, he supported himself on her arm. It was muscular and steady. She seemed calm, contented and harmonious. He was convinced he had once seen her crying.

CHAPTER 5

Jensen stood at the window with thin blue curtains and looked out over the lawn towards the road and factory. He had seen another camel a few days earlier.

He was wearing his own suit. They had removed the bandages and taken out the stitches and he could move relatively freely. The only thing that was still difficult was going to the toilet.

There was a knock at the door and he turned to see who it was. The doctor and nurse never knocked, and nor did the cleaning lady or the man who came to mend the WC that was always going wrong.

Nobody entered but the knock came again. Jensen went over to the door and opened it. Outside stood a small, grey-haired man in a dark blue suit and black felt hat. He had glasses and was carrying a black briefcase. The man immediately took off his hat and said:

'Inspector Jensen?'

'Yes.'

It was the first word he had spoken since reaching the airport three months earlier. He thought his voice sounded husky and alien.

'I've got a message for you. May I come in?' What the man said was grammatically correct, but he had a slight accent.

Jensen stepped aside.

'Be my guest.'

It was an effort to speak, and it almost disgusted him somehow.

The man took off his hat and opened his briefcase. He took out a pink telex strip and handed it to Jensen. The message was concise.

Return home immediately.

Jensen looked enquiringly at his visitor.

'Who sent this?'

'I don't know.'

'Why isn't it signed?'

'I don't know.'

The man hesitated for a moment.

'The communication came through diplomatic channels,' he said.

'Who are you?'

'I come from one of the sections of our Ministry of Foreign Affairs. I have never been to your country, but I studied the language at university.'

Jensen said nothing. Waited for the man to continue.

'We knew nothing about your state of health, not even whether you were still alive. I was sent here to deliver the message.'

Jensen still said nothing.

'Your doctor says you have quite recovered and can leave the hospital the day after tomorrow. There are just a few tests to do first.'

The man hesitated again. Then he said:

'Congratulations.'

'Thanks.'

'The doctor says they initially thought there was no hope for you.'

He produced an envelope from his briefcase.

'I have taken the liberty of reserving a seat for you on a plane leaving at 9 a.m. the day after tomorrow. Here are the tickets.'

Jensen took the envelope and put it away in his inside pocket.

'Did the communication say anything apart from those three words?'

More hesitation.

'Only some general instructions, such as how and where to find you.'

'Do you know who the communication came from?'

Pause.

'Yes.'

'Who?'

'I'm not permitted to tell you that.'

'Why not?'

'The sender of the message specifically asked me not to. It wasn't our idea, you see.'

'Wasn't it?'

'No.'

'But I have been given the task of relaying your answer to the person in question. Will you be flying home the day after tomorrow?'

'Yes,' said Jensen.

'Excellent,' said the man, picking up his hat. He went towards the door.

'Just a moment,' said Jensen. 'Have you been in contact with our embassy?'

The man had already half opened the door. He stopped, caught in mid movement.

'Your embassy is unmanned.'

'Unmanned?'
'Yes. There's nobody there.'
'Why not?'
'I don't know. Goodbye.'

CHAPTER 6

The nurse gave Jensen a lift to the airport. She was wearing open sandals and a strappy, red cotton dress. The road was full of potholes and it was a battered old car, but she drove fast and skilfully. Jensen was sitting in the back seat. He noted the sweat glistening on the back of her neck and between her shoulder blades. Out in the fields he saw tractors and combine harvesters. They passed through a village of low, mud houses. The village street was swarming with children and domestic animals. She constantly sounded her horn to chase chickens, goats and pigs out of the way. The children roared with laughter at her. She stuck her tongue out at them and they laughed even more.

The nurse had a luxuriant growth of black hair in her armpits. Outside the terminal building she stood on tiptoe and kissed him on the cheek.

The noise of the engine changed and the plane began its descent. Jensen looked at the clock. It was two hours earlier than expected. The seat-belt signs were switched on, the plane cut through the cloud cover, levelled out over misty fields and landed on a runway shiny with rain. Once the jet engines had whined to a stop, he looked out of the window.

He wasn't home yet. But he immediately recognised where he was and knew where they had landed. In a neighbouring country, not his own. He knew the language here and even spoke it tolerably well. The schedule had indicated it would be a non-stop flight. He remained in his seat.

After a while, an official of some kind came into the cabin and said:

'The plane will not continue its journey. All passengers are invited to disembark.'

He repeated the announcement in a number of languages. Apart from Jensen, there were only two other passengers on board.

Outside it was raining and the raw chill in the air caught him off guard. The arrivals hall was noisy and smoky, crammed with people drinking beer and talking over each other.

The woman at the information desk gave him a pitying look and said:

'There are no planes going there. All flights have been suspended until further notice.'

'Suspended?'

'Yes. All communications have been cut off.'

'Where can I telephone from?'

'Here. But there's no point. The phone lines aren't working either.'

'Why?'

'I don't know. Nobody knows for sure.'

At that moment, he heard his name being called over the public address system. The woman did a double take, and looked at his ticket again.

'Is your name Jensen?'

'Yes.'

'Follow me.'

She took him over to a lift and up to the top floor.

'Go to reception room four,' she said. 'They're expecting you.' Jensen walked along the carpeted corridor, reading the doors. He stopped at number four and knocked.

'Come in,' said a voice.

There were three men in the room. Two of them were slumped in comfortable armchairs. Their faces were drawn and pale. He did not know either of them. There was a third person over by the window, standing with his back to the door. As he turned round, Jensen recognised him. It was the man from the election posters. The man considered to represent the totally interdependent concepts of welfare, security and accord better than anyone else. He had been the Minister for the Interior when Jensen left, and ought to be head of government by now. His Excellency.

'Are you Jensen?' he said in a shrill, uncontrolled tone.

'Yes.'

'Sit down, for God's sake. Sit down.'

Inspector Jensen sat down.

CHAPTER 7

'I've heard about you, Jensen,' said His Excellency, the senior minister. 'You caused me a certain amount of inconvenience a few years back.'

He was plainly making an effort to keep his voice at a normal level. To sound as if things were as usual.

'Would you like a beer?' he asked abruptly.

'No, thank you.'

'They make damn good beer here, I must say.'

He sat down opposite Jensen. As he poured his own beer, his hands shook so much that he almost knocked the glass over.

'You know these gentlemen, of course?'

Jensen had never seen them before and had no idea who they were, even after the minister had introduced them by name. They were both members of the government.

'Someone said once that the distance between the people and those in authority was too great,' the senior minister mumbled to himself.

Jensen knew what he meant. The red-haired police doctor had once said:

'Can you think of anything more abstract and distant than God and the minister? Anything more remote?'

There was something in what he said. The Accord regime did not promote any kind of cult of the personality; that had been one of its founding principles. The general uniformity and smoothing out that was its goal did not allow for any positions of personal power other than those based on capital, which could be consolidated without the intervention of the public sector. For official functions there was always the Regent to call on. It was only in the last two elections that there had been a named candidate with a face, presumably so the relationship between people in general and the technocrats who exercised formal power should not get too unreal.

'Prime Minister . . .' said Jensen, but the man instantly interrupted him.

'I'm not the head of government. The election was . . . postponed.'

'Why?'

The minister stood up suddenly. He made a jerky sort of gesture, contemplated his trembling hands for a moment and then thrust them in his jacket pockets.

'Circumstances were such that it was considered appropriate to postpone the democratic elections,' he said stonily.

One of the other men cleared his throat and said:

'Inspector Jensen?'

'Yes.'

'Did you send in your declaration of loyalty?'

'Yes.'

'I told you there was no connection,' the minister said peevishly.

In the room, all was silent. Outside, the jet engines roared. Jensen looked at the men one after the other and said calmly:

'What's happened?'

'The incomprehensible thing is, we don't know. We don't know what's happened and above all, we don't know how it's happened. There's no logical connection between the details we do know.'

'What details?'

'Jensen, we need to take this from the beginning.'

'Yes. Why are we here?'

'I don't know.'

'You don't know? How did you get here?'

'The same way as you. On a plane. From abroad. We were on our way back from a ... state visit. But we couldn't get any further than this. All communications are severed.'

'Why are all communications severed?'

'We don't know. Nobody knows.'

'How long have you been here?'

'Three days.'

'Have you tried to get home by other means?'

His Excellency did not answer.

'You summoned me here, is that right?'

'Yes.'

'Why?'

'Jensen, we need to take things in order. Firstly, are you willing to take on the mission?'

'What mission?'

'Investigating what's happened. Since we don't know where we are, we can't give you any precise orders.'

'I know where we are.'

'You misunderstand me. I mean in a legal sense. As you may know, we haven't recognised the government in this country, for practical economic reasons. For us, it exists only as a geographical concept. We have no extraterritorial rights.'

'Why are we here, then?'

The minister threw out his arms.

'Where the hell do you want us to go? I ask you to do me a favour, do the country a favour, and you . . .'

He left the sentence unfinished. The member of the cabinet who had not yet spoken shook his head and said:

'Police. What did I tell you?'

The man was fairly young and had an arrogant, supercilious manner. Jensen recalled having heard his name a few times and knew he was one of the government's rising stars. He had held various ministerial positions and the general expectation was that he would head the government sooner or later. At present he was the Minister for Education. He had previously been head of communications, charged with the sensitive task of directing radio and television censorship.

Jensen regarded him without expression and said:

'I would just like to point out that I am not on active duty, that we are abroad, and that I have been given no concrete information whatsoever except what I was told at the airline desk.'

'Jensen, Jensen,' the senior minister said sorrowfully and imploringly. 'We know you are an extraordinarily skilful police officer.'

'Really?'

'Yes. The way you handled that embarrassing affair four and a half years ago admittedly made things even more embarrassing, but the investigation was technically perfect . . .'

'So perfect that it led to the deaths of thirty-two people, you mean?'

'Don't rake all that up again now.'

The Minister for Education said frostily:

'Mr Jensen, I hope you are aware that we can put you back on the beat the minute the situation returns to normal. We can also kick you out of the force altogether if we feel like it. You've caused trouble before.'

'Just so,' said the senior minister. 'You should think of your family, at the very least.'

'I haven't got one,' said Jensen.

'All right then, what is it you want? Money?'

'Facts.'

'I told you: there aren't any. We don't know what's happened.'

'Why were the elections postponed?' Jensen asked.

The senior minister gave a nervous shrug.

'As I said . . .'

The education expert jumped up and gave the senior minister a far from appreciative look.

'The election was postponed because of the serious disturbances that erupted in the closing stages of the campaign,' he said.

'Disturbances of what kind?'

'Riots. Running battles. The police and army were called in.'

'A revolt?' Jensen said doubtfully.

'Not at all. It was more a case of people turning with justified indignation on the nation's enemies within. Unfortunately they resorted to methods that were far too violent.'

'What happened then? Once the election had been postponed?'

'That is something we don't know with any certainty. Most of the government left the country at that point.'

'With their families?'

'Yes, they're safe.'

'And the Regent?'

'In a place of safety.'

'Why are all the borders closed?'

'As far as we are aware, the borders aren't closed at all.'

'But all communications are cut off?'

'Yes. Because a very serious epidemic is raging in the country. Here and in other foreign countries, they have accepted that theory.'

'And is there any factual proof that the theory is correct?'

'Yes. Before communications were broken off, the authorities requested medical help from abroad.'

'And?'

'Some personnel, mostly volunteer doctors and nurses from a number of foreign countries, immediately went on their own initiative. Soon after that, the message came through that the situation was under control and no further help was required.'

'And then?'

'Just after we had that message, communications were broken off.'

'When was that?'

'Five days ago. To be precise, I can tell you there has been no official contact for the past five days or nights.'

'But unofficially?'

'A few people have left the country. In groups of varying sizes. None of them we have been in touch with knows for sure what's happened.'

'Why did they leave the country?'

'Fear and uncertainty drove them to it. But . . .'

'Yes?'

'There are various indications to support the theory that an epidemic has broken out there. A number of people have died in hospitals abroad.'

'What of?'

'It's been impossible to establish the cause.'

'Are the border controls still working?'

'As you know, most of our borders are sea ones, and the land borders, as you also know, generally run through areas that are practically uninhabited. After much persuasion the police forces of neighbouring states agreed to reconnoitre outposts on our territory. Very unwillingly, I must say. Everyone's scared of the epidemic.'

'And?'

'The outposts proved to be unmanned.'

'What's happened to the foreign embassies?'

'A lot of them were evacuated during the disturbances. The police and army couldn't, or wouldn't, protect them.'

'Sounds unlikely.'

'It's true, nonetheless. The remaining residences were closed when the rumours of an epidemic started to spread.'

'What happened to the medical volunteer expeditions from other countries?'

'They haven't come back. And there's been no word from them.'

'Are the internal communications working?'

'Evidently not. Three military aircraft and one from the civil aviation side have crashed in foreign territory. Nobody knows why.'

Jensen sat in silence for a few moments. Then he said:

'Is this information correct?'

'Yes. Unfortunately.'

Nobody said a word. Jensen did not move a muscle.

'One more thing,' he said.

'What's that?'

'Could they all be dead?'

'No. We know there's considerable activity, particularly in the capital.'

'How do you know that?'

The Minister for Education glanced quickly at the senior minister, who gave a resigned shrug.

'I can't answer that question without giving away a military secret.'

Jensen said nothing.

'But I shall answer it, all the same. It so happens that a friendly superpower has been carrying out systematic, high-altitude surveillance operations over our country for a number of years. Its reconnaissance planes are fitted with comprehensive surveillance equipment. We have been able to share their observations through informal channels.'

'And?'

'As I say, there's no shortage of activity.'

'Military?'

'Not in the capital. There is, however, evidence of some military deployment in the countryside.'

'What's happening in the capital?'

'We don't know. But we know something's going on there.'

'Something organised?'

'Yes.'

Jensen went back to his starting point.

'Why are we here?'

The politician's reply was shockingly honest.

'Because no one wants anything to do with us.'

'Why don't you try to get home?'

'Because we daren't.'

CHAPTER 8

Jensen stood up and went over to the window. He stared out into the rain. Without turning round, he said:

'What do you intend to do?'

'Assign you the task of finding out as much as possible about what's happened.'

'You haven't the authority to assign me tasks here.'

'No. We know. But we're doing it anyway. We want you to try to get an overview of the situation as quickly as possible and report back here.'

'How?'

'We have certain contacts here. Since this country doesn't officially exist for us, we don't need to stick too rigidly to protocol. A helicopter will transport you to a particular point, which naturally you can choose for yourself. It will then return to the same place at a pre-appointed time and pick you up. You will come back here. You can be away three days at most, or find some other way to report back, otherwise . . .'

'What happens otherwise?'

'Otherwise we shall have to resort to different methods.'

'What sort of methods?'

Behind him he could hear the politicians muttering amongst themselves. He did not turn round but contented himself with waiting for their answer. It took about a minute or so.

'The friendly superpower that I referred to just now has

significant interests of both a political and an economic nature in keeping our country under surveillance. It is, however, extremely tied up in other parts of the world and has no wish to intervene without due cause, particularly not in the current confused situation. If, on the other hand, it turns out that antisocial elements are attempting to exploit the situation, then we can request . . . military assistance. I hope. On a limited scale. This superpower is, as I say, extremely committed else-where. But it will help us, we are sure of that. If it's politically expedient. Always assuming the antisocial elements don't manage to take over the administration, which is basically out of the question anyway.'

'What do you mean by antisocial elements?'

The answer was the only thinkable one.

'Communists.'

Silence. It had all gone quiet out on the airfield, too. The only sound was the rain.

'Well, Jensen. Will you go?'

'Yes.'

'Now? Right away?'

'Yes.'

'Excellent.'

Jensen made no reply.

'Are you armed?'

'No.'

'Perhaps you should be.'

'Why?'

'You never know. We'll take care of that detail.' Jensen still did not move.

'One more thing,' he said.

'What's that?'

'Immediately before I went on sick leave, I was ordered to arrest forty-three doctors working in my district, among them my own police doctor. I assume similar orders were issued to all districts.'

'We don't know anything about that,' His Excellency hastened to say. 'That's a police matter.'

'Could those arrests conceivably have anything to do with subsequent developments?' Jensen asked, unruffled.

'Definitely not,' said the Minister for Education.

'I've already said there was no connection,' said His Excellency.

Renewed silence. It was the minister who broke it. The minister was a youthful forty-year-old with blue eyes, a slight squint and an effeminate look around the mouth. He was clearly the one who made the decisions.

'Where do you plan to land?'

'The airport.'

'You haven't any imagination,' His Excellency said in a petulant, reproachful tone.

'That's right,' said Jensen. 'I haven't.'

CHAPTER 9

It was a jet-powered helicopter, but the journey was still a slow one. The weather conditions were poor, with mist and low, fast-moving cloud, and the ground remained largely out of sight. Violent gusty showers of rain and wet snow beat against the Plexiglas windscreen, and the pilot took the aircraft up to a less turbulent height.

Jensen stopped looking out. There was nothing to see. Instead he took out the gun that was weighing down his jacket pocket in an annoying manner.

The gun was a 7.65 millimetre Beretta pistol. It was old, but he had selected it because he was familiar with the mechanism. He had also been given three extra magazines and a brown leather holster.

Jensen hadn't fired a shot since he graduated from police college. He had kept his police-issue gun in the glove compartment of his car, but a few years before he had moved it to a locker at the police station. During his training he had been an excellent shot. He had once won a medal in a competition.

He pulled his suitcase towards him and opened it, put the pistol into the holster and placed them both neatly on top of his private possessions. Then he shut the lid and locked the case.

The helicopter had stopped lurching; the engine droned

evenly and soporifically. There was nothing to see but the clouds and the back of the pilot's leather jacket.

Jensen was no longer in pain. The skin around the operation scar was pulling a bit, and he felt weak. It didn't hurt any more. What remained was a strange emptiness, as if a close relative had died. For many years the pain had been his constant companion; now it was gone. The fact brought him no relief or satisfaction.

He fell asleep with his head leaning on the back rest of the seat.

The pilot woke him half an hour later.

'As far as I can tell, we're there.'

Outside the cockpit there was nothing to be seen but thick grey fog.

'The control tower isn't answering,' said the man at the controls. 'The radar isn't working. Visibility's almost zero and it'll soon be dark. Shall I try to land?'

'Yes.'

'This is going to be very dodgy. I suppose we'd better go down and have a look.'

Jensen nodded. He took his wallet out of his inside pocket, located his police ID badge and put it in his breast pocket.

The helicopter pilot gave him a surprised sideways glance. He was about thirty, a small man with unkempt hair and a frank, open face.

He had presumably thought Jensen was about to give him some money.

Below them, something was taking shape out of the fog.

'Uh-oh,' said the pilot. 'Right on top of the terminal. How about that for navigation? No lights, either.'

The machine pulled sharply back into the air. The fog closed in on them again.

'Okay, we'll try a bit further out on the airfield.'

He brought the machine down with the greatest of care. It took a minute or so, and then they could see the ground, the grass and the concrete landing strips. To their right, a red and white object emerged from the gloom.

'A tanker,' said the pilot. 'Parked right across the runway. They've blockaded the airport.'

He peered out into the fog.

'Here,' he said. 'This'll be fine.'

Jensen got up and put on his overcoat. He picked up his hat.

The helicopter touched down. The pilot reached out an arm and opened the cabin door.

'Can you see the landing beacon over there? There's a number on it. A black four. We'll take that as a landmark.'

He looked at his watch.

'The day after tomorrow and the day after that I'll be here at exactly nine in the morning. I'll wait for two minutes. From 09.00 to 09.02.'

Jensen took his suitcase and climbed out on to the ground.

'Bye,' said the helicopter pilot. 'Best of luck.'

'Goodbye.'

The machine took off in a roaring swirl of air and was swallowed by the mist. The engine sound died away.

The silence was then complete. There was nothing to see. It was starting to get dark and the visibility was worsening still further.

Inspector Jensen put on his hat and set off towards the terminal building.

CHAPTER 10

When Jensen reached the terminal, it was almost dark. The big glass doors were locked. There were no lights on, and nothing to indicate there was any living being in the vicinity.

On the concrete forecourt were six baggage trucks and a tank painted in camouflage colours. Its crew had left it without even stopping to close the hatch. He climbed up and looked in. Everything seemed normal.

Out on the airfield he had seen the burnt-out wreck of a crashed passenger plane, and numerous lorries and army buses lined up across the runways.

He walked round the outside of the building and came to a tall wire fence. He followed it until he came to a gate. It was locked. Jensen threw over his suitcase and climbed after it. As he launched himself at the ground, the sleeve of his coat caught in the barbed wire on top. A long rip was torn in it. He stood there in the dark, feeling along the fabric with his fingers. The damage seemed irreparable.

Jensen worked his way back along the fence until he reached the front of the terminal building.

The street lights weren't working. It was entirely dark and he had to feel his way along the wall. The air was raw and cold, and it was drizzling. He stopped and tried to get his bearings. He did not know the airport very well, but he had a good memory. From what he could remember, he was less than ten metres from the main entrance. Outside it there were telephone boxes and a taxi rank. He left the wall, crossed the pavement and walked into the side of a car. Found the handle and opened the front door. When he reached his hand in, it came up against something soft.

Jensen knew at once what it was. It did not make him jump. He was neither scared nor surprised, but put down his case and began feeling around with both hands. He confirmed there was a dead body slumped over the steering wheel.

He shut the car door, picked up his case and cut back across the pavement. The phone boxes were where he had expected to find them. He went into the first, fished a coin out of his pocket. He heard the coin fall into place, but got no tone in the receiver. The telephone was unusable. He moved on to the next one. Same thing there.

Jensen had just gone into the third phone box when he heard the howl of a siren. It started somewhere not too far away and approached at speed. Within a few minutes, the beam of light from a pair of headlamps cut through the mist and drizzle. The vehicle braked and came to a stop with its front wheels on the pavement and its headlights directed on the terminal building, no more than fifteen metres from the phone boxes. The glare was reflected by the wall of glass, shedding a diffuse light. Through the steamed-up glass of the phone box he could see that the vehicle was a standard ambulance, white with a red cross on the side and a flashing blue light on top. The siren stopped wailing and the ignition was turned off, but the headlights were left on and the rotating light on the roof continued to cast its flashes of blue lightning into the darkness. Two people in white coats got out.

Jensen picked up his suitcase and was about to push open the swing door when he stopped.

Both had blue armbands and one was a woman. He had never seen a female stretcher-bearer before. He froze, listening.

'They must have heard wrong,' said the woman. 'Could anyone really land in this weather?'

'Seems pretty unlikely, but we'd better check.'

They switched on their torches and went in separate directions. The woman passed close by the telephone box. Jensen remained motionless. Her movements were quick and elastic. She seemed quite young. The sound of her footsteps faded away. It was quiet for a moment. Then the steps approached again.

'Hello?' called the woman.

'Yes?'

'Bring your torch over here. There's a dead body in this car.'

The ambulance man passed right by the phone box, too. Jensen couldn't see them any longer, but he could hear their voices clearly.

'Some old bloke,' the man said sadly. 'Fancy sitting here dying in your taxi outside a barred and bolted airport. He had his cap on, too.'

'Very odd that people can't learn to do as they're told,' said the woman.

'We'll have to take him with us to the central unit.'

'Yep. Give me a hand here.'

'Hadn't I better get a stretcher?'

'No need. I'm stronger than I look.'

'Hey, hang on a minute.'

'Yes, what is it?'

'This old guy's sick.'

'Well, he's dead.'

'I know that, but look at him. He's blue. Must have had a heart attack.'

'Well we'll take him to the central unit anyway.'

They carried the dead man to the ambulance, opened the back doors and heaved in the body. The woman wiped her forehead with the sleeve of her coat and looked about.

'Have you got treatment tonight?' she said.

'Yes, at twelve.'

'Good. We'll have time for sex beforehand, just a quickie.'

'Fine by me. What did you say your name was?'

'I didn't.'

They climbed into the front of the ambulance again, the engine started and the ambulance backed off in a wide arc, its headlights sweeping across the immediate surroundings. Jensen saw there were three cars parked a little way off.

One was a police patrol car.

The ambulance drove off. The growl of the engine was soon drowned out by the noise of the rain, but then the siren began to wail again.

The sound receded.

Jensen waited until it was completely silent. Then he left the phone box and walked purposefully towards where he had seen the police car parked. He knew that model well and as long as there was petrol in the tank he'd be able to jump-start it.

But there was no need. The car was unlocked and the key had been left in the ignition. He switched on the interior light and could see nothing special or unusual. The tank was almost full. The glove compartment contained a half-empty packet of cigarettes, a pistol and a torch. He looked at the patrol car number below the dashboard. As he had guessed, it belonged to the police unit stationed at the airport.

The engine started at once. He switched on the headlights, left the airport and joined the motorway, driving moderately fast. After about twenty minutes an ambulance came speeding up behind him with its blue light flashing and its siren on. As it tried to overtake, Jensen put his foot down and had soon left it far behind. A while after that, he met an oncoming grey bus and two more ambulances. They passed so fast that he had no time to register any details.

The rain got heavier and the visibility grew worse than ever. In one place, however, he thought he could see flickering lights in the windows of a tower block in one of the self-clearance areas. He was only three kilometres from the district where he lived when he met a roadblock improvised out of a row of lorries, parked close together and blocking the motorway.

In the middle of the roadblock a big, crudely painted sign announced: INFECTION RISK – HELP STATION 4KM – FOLLOW ROUTE 73. Under the words was a painted arrow, pointing to the right. Jensen saw the roadblock so late that he only just had time to stop. Some earlier motorist had not been so lucky, for he saw the crushed wreck of a little car jammed between the big lorries.

He backed away from the abandoned lorries and turned down the slip road leading off the motorway. He passed a few more signs directing people to the help station, but soon turned off route 73 on to a narrow back road.

Inspector Jensen was entirely at home in the area, but it still took him a couple of hours to find a back way into the estate where he lived. The torrential rain made observation impossible. He parked in his usual place. Took with him the pistol, the torch and the patrol car log, which was where it should be, in the compartment under the driving seat. He locked the car, took the suitcase out of the boot and went up to his flat. Neither the lift nor the stairwell lighting was working. Nor were the lights in the flat.

There wasn't a sound in the entire building.

He switched on the torch and looked round. Everything seemed untouched.

On the floor just inside the door lay four messages, obviously posted through the letterbox. Two of them were printed, the others run off on a duplicating machine.

The moment he bent down to pick them up, the torch went out. He shook it several times, to no avail. He didn't have another one, nor any alternative way of getting light.

He looked at the luminous hands on his watch. It was five past midnight. His mission was already entering its second day.

It was pitch dark in the flat. He felt his way over to the bed, took off his hat, coat, jacket, tie and shirt.

Jensen was extremely tired. He had been travelling for many hours.

The raw, damp cold in the room indicated that the heating was not working either.

He lay on his back in the bed and wrapped himself in the blanket. Turned on his side and pulled up his knees.

In the far distance he could hear sirens.

He wondered if the couple in the ambulance had fitted in their quickie.

CHAPTER 11

Jensen was wide awake the moment he opened his eyes. Grey dawn light was filtering into the room. His first thoughts were that he had ruined his best overcoat and that he wanted a wash. He got up and went to the bathroom. There was no water in the taps. The toilet did work, however. Once.

He stroked the stubble on his chin with the tips of his fingers. Since he only had an electric razor, there wasn't much he could do.

Jensen went back to the bedroom, took the rest of his clothes off, took out some clean socks and underwear. Plus a new white shirt. He dressed quickly but carefully, and combed his hair in front of the mirror.

He was hungry and cold and went out to the kitchen, but the refrigerator was empty. He had emptied it three months earlier and set it to defrost. In the wardrobe he had two bottles of spirits hidden behind his police caps on the top shelf but he did not feel like drinking alcohol. He went through the kitchen cupboards systematically and found a jar of honey. It was all he had to eat, and since the alcohol was all he had to drink, he fetched one of the bottles from the wardrobe and poured about ten centilitres into a tumbler. He drank it in gulps, accompanied by about a third of the jar of honey.

Then he went into the bedroom and got his binoculars out of the chest of drawers. Took up position by the window and started scanning the area. The rain had eased off but it was misty and hard to see much. He trained the binoculars on the apartment block opposite, adjusted the focus and ran his eyes along the rows of windows. Everything looked completely normal, but there were no lights on anywhere and it took him a long time to detect any signs of activity. Finally he saw a curtain move at a window on the seventh floor, and just after that, he saw a face. It was a woman. Almost immediately a man also came into view behind the windowpane. Their faces looked pale and strange. Perhaps it was because of the distance or the poor visibility. They looked out for only a couple of seconds, then vanished. No further movement was to be seen in the flat. Jensen measured the position of the window with his eye and calculated the position of the room in relation to the front entrance door. Staircase C, seventh floor, first door on the left.

He continued his inspection, and gradually noticed a few other details to indicate that the block was lived in. Blurred little movements, the twitch of a curtain, reflections in the windows. At a guess, there were people in maybe a third of the flats.

He heard a faint engine sound and when he pointed the binoculars the other way he saw a bus being driven along the motorway. It was coming from the direction of the city. As far as he could see, there were no passengers aboard, but the mist made it very hard to be certain. Right after the bus, he glimpsed two other vehicles going by. Presumably ambulances with their sirens and emergency lights turned off.

Jensen put the binoculars down on the window ledge, went through to the bedroom and got his overcoat. Studied the rip, which was a good twenty centimetres long, folded up the garment and put it on the hall table. He selected a different coat from the wardrobe and hung it in the hall. Then he picked up the sheets of duplicated paper from the hall carpet and put them on his bedside table along with the logbook of the patrol car.

Then he sat down and started to read. First the logbook. He skipped forward to the day he had left the country and then went quickly through, glancing at every page. To begin with he found nothing unusual or startling. The six policemen who used the car had worked in pairs in three shifts, and signed the notes with their service numbers. These were the same numbers as were embossed on their police badges, which they were obliged to wear on the left-hand side of their uniform jackets, where they would be fully visible. This rule applied to all uniformed officers with the exception of those in positions of command. The six constables' numbers were: 80, 315, 104, 405, 103 and 601. As was customary, they were divided up so that a younger officer, with a higher service number, was paired with an older and more experienced colleague. There were basically only three types of entry in the log. The arrest of drunks, traffic accidents, and suicides or attempted suicides.

Jensen found the first alarming entry on the page dated 30 September. Number eighty who had been keeping the log between 4 p.m. and midnight had noted the following:

16.46 ordr km 9 s mwy dem 2 arr tkn 9 dist 19.05 pce rstrd rtn stn

So at fourteen minutes to five that day, the patrol car had been ordered to kilometre marker number nine on the southern motorway to police a demonstration. Two people had been arrested and taken to the Ninth District police station. It had taken until 19.05, that is to say over two hours from the time the order was given, for peace to be restored and the car to return to its base.

Kilometre marker nine was very close to the city centre. It was extremely surprising for a police car to be sent there all the way from the airport.

Jensen began scrutinising the log more carefully and with greater interest. Over the week that followed there were two similar entries, and after that the frequency increased sharply, while entries about the arrest of drunks became fewer and fewer. They clearly hadn't had any spare time for dealing with alcoholics.

Suicide cases, which at the start of the log had featured at a rate of two or three a week, appeared only sporadically.

As the patrol's duties became more sensational in nature, the officers had abandoned the usual cryptic abbreviations in their reports and went over to short entries in more or less standard prose. The log entries started getting more slapdash and less precise. Words like disturbances, scuffles and riots appeared on every page. They had clearly been summoned to the city centre and its environs on a daily basis. On the page for 2 November there was an entry of just six words:

Serious disturbances. Shots fired. Military assistance.

Exactly three weeks before, the phrase *patient transport*, later shortened to *pt trs*, was used for the first time. That meant the regular ambulance service could no longer cope with serious cases of illness and had had to ask the police to step in. After that, there were several patient transports every day.

Then the phrase suddenly disappeared. Others appeared in its place. The centre, the district hospital, the main hospital. Time after time. From the twenty-fifth onwards, officer 405 had kept the log single-handed. Jensen studied the remaining pages. The twenty-fifth had been a Monday.

Monday. Central Unit. Main hosp. Nos. 104 and 405 did not report for work.
Tuesday: No. 80 died in car. Drove him to unit.
Wednesday: State of emergency. Ordered to stay at airport.
Thursday: Sent to assist blockading of runway.
Friday: Police radio not functioning. 81st district unmanned.
Saturday: Sent to main hosp. section C. Bus.

That was the last entry in the car's logbook. It was five days old. Jensen went back and read the entries for the previous month through again. Then he shut the log and laid it aside.

There was the distant wail of a siren. The sound came nearer. He went over to the window, put the binoculars to his eyes and trained them on the motorway. The visibility was as poor as ever; the rain seemed to be getting heavier again. About thirty seconds elapsed and then an ambulance loomed out of the mist. It was not going particularly fast, but its flashing light was on. Fifty metres behind it came a grey bus, presumably the one he had seen earlier. And after that came another ambulance.

It looked as though the bus was crammed with people. The convoy was heading north, towards the city.

He turned the binoculars rapidly to the windows in the apartment block next door, where he had seen the two faces a short while before. Detected a slight movement in a curtain, as if someone had pulled it a few centimetres to one side to view the road.

He went back to his bedside table, read the four notes that had come through the door and arranged them in chronological order.

The first read:

A serious epidemic has broken out in the city. All gatherings are therefore banned. Meetings of more than three people are not permitted. All citizens except those who work in the state administration are to remain in their homes. Schools and all private workplaces with more than three employees will close immediately. Make sure you have supplies of food. There is no need to panic. Medical assistance has been summoned and is on its way. Observe the highest standards of hygiene. Communications, radio, TV and telephone will not function fully. Avoid jamming the phone lines with unnecessary calls. The first symptoms of the epidemic are as follows: tiredness, dizziness, a severe headache, reddish flickering before the eyes. If you believe you or any member of your family to be infected, go immediately to the nearest help station. The nearest help station will be at the district school in the area where you live. It is strictly forbidden to leave the city. PLEASE NOTE! Panic will only help to spread the infection!

The announcement was dated the fifteenth of November and signed by the Minister for Public Health.

The next announcement was from the same authority and had been sent a week later, on the twenty-first of November. It read:

The current epidemic has been contained, but the situation remains grave. Continue to follow earlier instructions.

Further announcements will be made via loudspeaker vans. Electricity and water supplies can only be maintained on a limited basis. Fill bathtubs and other containers with drinking water. Save electric power. Healthy individuals licensed to give blood are urged to go to their local help station or the main hospital, Section C. PLEASE NOTE! Avoid any form of panic!

The other two communications differed in significant ways from the Public Health Ministry's exhortations. The paper was of a different kind and size. They were not printed but had been run off on a duplicating machine. Their tone was also different. Neither was dated, but by cross-referring to the entries in the patrol car logbook Jensen thought he could establish that the first had been sent on the previous Wednesday, i.e. the twenty-seventh of November. The text was brief and blunt:

State of emergency in force from midnight tonight. Total curfew to be imposed with the exception of two groups: the sick and blood donors. The sick are to go to their district help station or directly to the Central Detoxification Unit, km marker 6 on motorway 2. Blood donors are to attend the district help station or go to the main hospital. For further details apply to the block security official.

The announcement was clearly local. It was signed by someone who contented himself with just a title: Head District Consultant.

Jensen heard vehicle engines, went to the window and snatched up the binoculars. Three military trucks were moving north on the motorway. They appeared to be heavily laden. The backs were covered in tarpaulin.

He looked at the clock. One minute to eight. Went back to read the other duplicated announcement.

Epidemic now under control. State of emergency still in force. From today, total, round-the-clock curfew to be observed. This applies also to the sick and to blood donors, who are to remain at home and await further instructions. Infringements of the curfew are a risk to public health and offenders will be strictly prosecuted.

This communication was also undated, and signed by the Head District Consultant.

Jensen unpacked his case.

He put the two handguns next to each other on the bed and stood contemplating them.

The service pistol that he had taken from the police car was the better weapon, a 9 millimetre modified Parabellum. The Beretta, on the other hand, was lighter and less bulky.

He left both guns lying there, put a ballpoint pen and a new notebook in his pocket instead, donned his coat and hat and went out of the flat. On his way downstairs, he threw his torn overcoat down the rubbish chute.

CHAPTER 12

Inspector Jensen walked with measured steps, cutting across the car park and children's play area. The playhouses looked like transparent plastic igloos. The only problem with them was that there were hardly any children in the area, even under normal circumstances.

The front entrance door and the narrow stairwell were identical to those in the block where he lived. The lighting was not working. Nor was the lift. He set off up the cramped, winding stairs. Stopped halfway to get his breath back. Listened. He knew there were people in a few of the flats, at the very least, and that the block was as shoddily built as his own, with very thin walls. Even so, he could not pick up a single sound to indicate human life.

On the seventh floor he stopped, looked all round and tapped very lightly on one of the doors. No reaction.

Jensen waited for a while, then knocked again. Harder this time. There was still nothing to be heard.

Jensen thumped the door heavily with his fist and said:

'Police. Open up.'

This time he thought he could make out a sound from inside the flat. It sounded like a stifled sob. Or perhaps just a short, gasping intake of breath.

Jensen looked at the door. He could probably get it open. Under the alcohol law now in force, the police had formal authority to enter private property. On his key ring he had a number of universal tools with which he ought to be able to open conventional locks to standard housing and places of work. The law had a whole series of supplementary paragraphs, exceptions and special provisions, all formulated in the vaguest of terms. It also outlawed the fitting of bolts and special locks to apartment doors. This applied under normal circumstances. Where the dividing line ran between normal and other circumstances was never clearly stated, but there was a very simple rule of thumb to help in the decision-making process. This was a normal residential area and a normal door and he was very probably capable of opening it. But before he could do so, he had to suspect that a crime had been committed.

There were sudden sounds of activity from the flat. Large, heavy objects were dragged across the floor and thumped against the door from the inside. The people who lived in the flat were barricading the entrance.

Jensen turned and went back down the stairs. Even three floors below, he could still hear something, presumably furniture, being shifted and piled up.

The door opened inwards. He was convinced he could have forced it anyway.

The rain was still drumming outside, peaceful and soothing. The mistiness persisted and the cloud height seemed no more than two hundred feet.

Inspector Jensen paused briefly and looked about him. The patrol car was where he had left it the night before.

The patrol car was intended for police use only, and built for the purpose. It was bulletproof with unpuncturable tyres. It could be locked from the inside and had two sets of radio equipment, a built-in tape player and a specially tuned engine.

Jensen was very familiar with its construction. He went up to it, unlocked the door and sat behind the steering wheel. Tried out the tape player. It was working, but there was nothing recorded on the tape. He fiddled with the radio equipment for a while. That worked, too, to the extent that he could hear a faint buzzing in the ether on the police frequency. That was all. He switched off the set, started the car, drove up on to the motorway and carried on northwards towards the city centre.

Although he had the highway to himself, he did not hurry.

When he had been on the road for about twenty minutes, he heard the blare of a horn. A white ambulance came into view in the rearview mirror about fifty metres behind him. Jensen did not accelerate and the other vehicle approached at speed and continued sounding its horn. When it drew level with him he could see two men in white coats in the front seats. The one at the wheel signalled to him with impatient gestures, but Jensen ignored him. The ambulance did not overtake but started forcing him over to the side of the road. The manoeuvre was not executed with much skill, and it was a good two minutes before he was obliged to brake and stop to avoid a collision. The other vehicle stopped, too, at an angle across his path. Jensen turned off the ignition, but remained in his seat. He saw now that this was no regular ambulance, but a delivery van that had been painted white, with crude red crosses on the sides and the rear doors. The two men got out and walked towards the patrol car.

They were wearing blue armbands, but were otherwise dressed entirely in white. White coats, white trousers and white clogs.

One was tall, with his hair brushed back and a short, neat,

dark beard. Grey-blue eyes and black horn-rimmed glasses. His expression was solemn and his look was earnest.

The other one was small and weedy, with a thin face and straight hair combed over to one side. A stray strand of dark hair had fallen down over his forehead. His full lips were stretched in an unsure, artificial-looking smile. The look in his brown eyes was distant and seemed fixed on something, presumably the other man's shoes or a point on the ground.

The tall one tried to pull open the car door. He couldn't. He made another impatient gesture and started to say something. Jensen pointed to the other side of the car, reached out a hand and pressed a button. The side window opened about ten centimetres. The men from the ambulance went round the car.

'Are you sick or healthy?' demanded the tall one.

'Healthy.'

'We need to take a closer look at you. Get out.'

Jensen didn't reply. The man gave him a severe look.

'Did you hear what I said?'

'Yes.'

'Get out.'

The man whose eyes were looking the wrong way plucked at his colleague's coat sleeve, pointed vaguely and said something. His voice was so quiet and indistinct that Jensen could not make out the words. The tall one listened, and nodded gravely.

'Why are you driving around in a police car?'

'Because I'm a policeman.'

Jensen showed his badge.

'Then you must be sick,' the tall man said categorically.

'We'll take care of you,' whispered the other one, not looking at Jensen. 'It could be serious.'

'Yes, it could be serious,' the tall one reiterated firmly.

'I'm healthy,' said Jensen. 'Who are you?'

'Doctors.'

'Can you show me your ID?'

The two men moved as though synchronised. They produced two laminated plastic cards and held them up. Jensen nodded. Their ID appeared to be genuine.

'You're breaking the curfew,' said the tall man. 'We must take you in hand.'

'We must take you in hand,' whispered his colleague.

'I hardly think so,' said Jensen. 'I'm a police officer.'

'What's your rank?'

'Inspector.'

'The police have no authority. And in any case, you're sick.'

'Who is in charge, then?' asked Jensen.

'The medical authorities.'

'Who is your immediate superior?'

'The chief medical officer.'

'The chief medical officer?'

The man with the smile and the cowed look whispered something else indistinguishable.

'Quite right,' said the tall one. 'We don't need to answer your questions. There's a state of emergency in force. You've broken the current regulations; you're a hazard to public safety.'

Jensen said nothing.

'You're seriously ill and we are going to take care of you. Don't be afraid.'

'Don't be afraid,' the other one repeated in a low voice. He fished in the pocket of his white coat and brought out a syringe. Fingered it and said in a pondering tone, as if directing the question to himself:

'What's his blood group?'

'What's your blood group?' asked the tall one, sterner than ever.

'Rhesus negative,' said Jensen.

The man with the syringe appeared to brighten up for a moment.

'Excellent,' he said to himself. 'Excellent. Now make him get out.'

'Get out,' said the tall one.

Jensen sat there in silence.

'We have extraordinary authority. The epidemic must be stopped. I'm sure you understand that. Do as we say. Obey.'

'Where are you going to take me?'

'To the main hospital,' said the tall one.

'Section C,' mumbled his colleague.

'I can find my own way there.'

'Come on out now. We haven't got time for all this.'

'Rhesus negative,' mumbled the little one, fingering the syringe.

'We've got more important things to do,' said the tall one.

'Fine,' said Jensen. 'Goodbye.'

He reached over and pressed the button.

The window slid upwards and closed. The man with the syringe jumped, and then started to wrench wildly at the door handle. His colleague with the severe look took him by the arm to calm him down, and began to walk towards the ambulance. The little one looked back over his shoulder with a crafty expression.

The two doctors got into the front seat without shutting the doors and started doing something. A moment later, Jensen saw the bearded man holding a microphone up to his mouth, moving his lips.

He immediately flicked a switch on the dashboard to activate the frequency finder. Within fifteen seconds, he had located the right wavelength. It was apparently less time than the man in the ambulance had taken to get through.

'Main hospital, over. Main hospital, over . . . Damn, they're not answering. No wait, here we go.'

There was a sudden blare from the radio. A male voice said in a distant croak:

'Main hospital here. Over.'

'Vehicle 300 here.'

'Yes? Where are you?'

'South motorway, at . . .'

Loud crackling. Jensen lost contact. He retuned. It took about thirty seconds, but then he could make out their voices again.

'A police car?'

'Yes.'

'A police inspector?'

'Yes.'

'Bring him straight here.'

'He refuses to come.'

'Are you armed?'

'Yes. We've got a pistol. But . . .'

'Yes? But what?'

'We don't know how to use it.'

'Idiots.'

There was a brief pause. Then the voice said irritably:

'Okay. We'll send a sanitary patrol. Keep him there.'

Jensen started his engine and backed rapidly away from the ambulance.

'He's clearing off,' the ambulance man said in dismay.

Jensen was already passing them. In the rearview mirror he saw the white van start to move.

'He's getting away.'

'Which way's he heading?'

'North.'

'No problem. Follow him. He'll have to stop at the entrance to the communication tunnel. He won't get any further.'

Jensen stepped on the gas and the ambulance disappeared into the drizzle. At the next exit he turned right and left the motorway.

A quarter of an hour later, he heard another exchange on the radio.

'That policeman . . .'

'Yes?'

'He's vanished.'

The voice was graver than ever, but seemed to have lost some of its severity. This time it was a woman who answered.

'It doesn't matter,' she said nonchalantly. 'He can't get into the restricted zone, whatever happens.'

'We need to get back now.'

'You do that. Don't sound so worried.'

CHAPTER 13

Inspector Jensen avoided residential areas and the main through roads. He crossed extensive industrial areas and scrubby expanses of undeveloped land that the speculators had not yet been able to exploit. All the factories and workshops looked deserted, and the only living creatures he saw were birds. The route he had chosen took him past, and at one point through, the central refuse tip, and the closer he got, the more birds there were. Mainly black and white ones. He was a policeman, not an ornithologist, and could not work out precisely what species they might be. There was nothing out of the ordinary, however, about their presence there.

Despite the rain, fires were burning here and there among the piles of refuse as usual, and the stench was disgusting. As soon as he had passed through the areas, the number of birds decreased.

The radio was still on, but he had heard nothing more. It was possible that the ambulances and the hospital communicated on a number of frequencies.

Jensen drove through a stretch of woodland littered with sparse, stunted conifers. A large number of the trees were dead, and only the tops of those that were still alive were a dull, dusty green. The road was narrow and potholed. It was rarely used these days, and nobody bothered to maintain it. He slowed down, and when he reached the edge of the wood he braked to a stop.

Jensen knew exactly where he was. In the Twenty-First police district, just on the city boundary. If the city centre really was shut off, this would be the critical bit of the journey. The road led uphill, to an elevated stretch. Beyond it lay a standard housing area consisting of six blocks of flats, a bus stop, a little supermarket and several kiosks. The buildings were lined up along one side of a wide street. Along the opposite side ran a high railway embankment, with tracks leading to the refuse tip. Officially, this was a dead end, but it had a link through to the road Jensen was on. Everyone who lived in the district knew about it. Everyone with any pretensions to knowing the layout of the city ought to be aware of it, too.

Jensen got out of the car and locked it. He left the road and walked uphill. On the brow of the hill there were a few straggly bushes. He stopped behind them and looked out over the area. The six sterile tower blocks stood mutely in the drizzle. The supermarket windows had been smashed, and there was an abandoned bus parked at the terminal stop. He could not detect any signs of life, either in the apartment blocks or in the short, wide street, whose whole length he was able to see. There was no roadblock there, at any rate, and he knew it was practically impossible to block all the roads leading to the centre beyond that point.

Jensen was just turning to go back to the car when he thought he saw a movement inside the supermarket. He stopped, stood still and waited. A few seconds later he saw it again, and shortly afterwards a figure climbed out through the hole smashed in the window.

The individual in question was a child. A small child, clad in a bright yellow mackintosh, blue trousers and red wellingtons. The distance was too great for him to make out whether it was a boy or a girl. The child had something in its hand, and zigzagged at a run towards the tower block nearest the rise and the edge of the wood.

Jensen moved swiftly down to the windowless end of the block, arriving while the child was still between the car park and the building. He peered round the corner and saw a little boy trotting along the footpath. The item in his hand was a cellophane bag of brightly coloured sweets. The boy was pigeon-toed, and far too busy gazing at his sweets to concentrate on walking properly. A couple of times he appeared almost to trip over his own feet.

The boy looked about four years old, five at most. He went into the last block, only five metres from the corner. He was so small that he had to lean all his weight against the heavy front door to get it open.

Jensen moved rapidly along the wall and went in after him. He could hear the child's footsteps on the stairs above him.

CHAPTER 14

For a few seconds, Inspector Jensen stood motionless outside
the door to the flat. Not a sound was to be heard from inside.
But he knew the boy with the bag of sweets had entered a
minute or so before. He also knew that someone had been
standing at the door, which had presumably been just slightly
open, and had pulled the boy into the hall. That someone had
whispered several reprimands. The voice had sounded hoarse
and tense.

Jensen had been half a flight of stairs below. He had moved
with care and presumed he had not been seen or heard.

He tapped lightly on the panel of the door with the knuckles
of his right hand. The reaction was instantaneous. Short, quick
steps thudded across the floor. Then the letterbox was opened
from the inside. Through the slit, about three centimetres wide,
Jensen could see a pair of surprised, greeny-blue eyes shaded
by thick eyelashes, long and blond. The little boy was kneeling
on the other side of the door, peeping out at him through the
flap of the letterbox.

'It's a man,' the boy said in a clear voice.

'Get away from that door, now. This minute.'

It was a woman's voice.

'It's a man,' the boy said again. 'He's standing out there.'

'Come here. Come here, for God's sake,' the woman said
desperately.

Jensen knocked once more, considerably harder this time. The letterbox flap fell shut with a bang. Someone dragged the child away from the door.

'Open up,' said Jensen.

After a long silence, the woman spoke again.

'Who is it?'

'Police. Open up.'

Another silence. Finally the woman said:

'What do you want?'

'I saw the child stealing goods from the shop. Open up.'

Jensen knocked on the door one last time. Nobody answered.

'If you don't open the door voluntarily I shall come in anyway.'

He heard the people inside changing position and moving away, as fast and soundlessly as they could.

Jensen got out his keys. The lock was of standard construction and he selected one of the skeleton keys without hesitation, inserted it in the lock and turned it. A faint metallic click announced that the door was no longer locked. He gave it a gentle push and it swung inwards with a faint squeak of the hinges. The curtains were closed, but still let in enough light to allow him to make out the essential details. The flat was the same as his own and equipped with roughly the same standard furniture. The woman was standing in the middle of the floor, almost as if paralysed. The boy was beside her. She was holding him firmly by the hand. The child stared at Jensen but appeared largely untroubled.

Jensen stood motionless, looking into the flat. Through the patter of the rain outside he could make out the sound of someone holding their breath, just to his right.

'You there,' he said. 'Step away from the door and go over to the others.'

The woman looked even more terrified. Her grip on the boy's hand tightened. Jensen took out his ID badge.

'Step away from the door and go and stand with the others,' he said. 'That's an order and I won't say it again.'

Almost immediately there was a deep sigh of resignation and a man who had been pressed to the wall beside the door stepped out into the room. He went to the other side of the boy, turned round and regarded Jensen dejectedly. The man was short in stature. He was in his stockinged feet, and dressed in trousers and an unbuttoned shirt. He had a hammer in his hand.

Jensen held up his ID badge.

'Inspector Jensen,' he said, 'Sixteenth District. I'm engaged in an investigation and want to talk to you.'

'Police,' the man said mistrustfully. 'Investigation?'

'He doesn't understand,' the woman said quickly, on a rising note of despair. 'He's so little. Only four. He doesn't understand.'

'Put the hammer down,' said Jensen.

Without taking his eyes off Jensen, the man bent down and laid the tool on the floor very carefully, as if not wanting to make any undue noise. His look was one more of apathy and fear than of resolution or hatred.

'He can get dressed by himself and he's learnt how to open the door,' the woman said. 'He's used to running out to play whenever he likes. Today he slipped out while I was in the kitchen, and we didn't have time to stop him.'

She stopped and looked at Jensen in alarm.

'He's only little,' she repeated.

'Are you his parents?'

'Yes.'

'Parents are responsible for supervising young children.'

'Yes, but . . .'

'Why didn't you go after the child and bring him back?'

The man looked at Jensen in astonishment.

'We didn't dare.'

Jensen stepped over the threshold and closed the door after him.

'He's alone,' the man said to himself under his breath. 'I should've killed him.'

The flat stank of urine, refuse and excrement. The people inside did not seem to be aware of it.

'The air's very bad in here,' Jensen remarked.

'Well nothing works, does it?' said the woman. 'No water, no light, no way of flushing the toilet. And we daren't open the windows, of course.'

Jensen got out his pen and notepad.

'Why not?'

'How can you ask that,' said the man. 'Don't you know what's happened?' Jensen did not reply.

'The sickness. Haven't you heard about it?'

'Have you or anyone in your family gone down with this sickness?'

'No.'

'Do you know anyone who has caught it?'

'Yes. Some people who lived round here. Not that we knew them.'

'What happened to them?'

'They went to hospital, of course. Well, one of them died before the ambulance got here. He was a policeman, as a matter of fact.'

'And it's the risk of infection that means you daren't go out?'

The man looked uncertainly at Jensen.

'I think so,' said the woman.

'You think so?'

'We're not allowed to go out,' she said. 'It's not permitted.'

'But people aren't prohibited from opening their doors?'

'No,' the man said hesitantly. 'But . . .'

'But what?'

'I didn't think you were from the police. I . . .'

He stopped. The little boy piped up instead:

'Are you a Mister Policeman?'

'Yes,' said Jensen gravely. 'I'm a policeman.'

'We haven't seen any police for weeks,' said the woman. 'We didn't think there were any left.'

Jensen turned back to the man.

'Where do you work?'

'The public cleansing department. At the central refuse tip. Until all this started.'

'What?'

'First it was a load of rumours about this awful disease. Then there was an announcement that the risk of infection was too serious for people to carry on going to work, except for the vital services. Why are you asking me all this?'

'Because I don't know,' said Jensen. 'I've been away.'

'Oh, I see,' the man said sceptically.

'How did you get the announcements?'

'On a printed leaflet that everyone got through their door. It was on TV, too. The TV was still working then, at least ours was. That was the fifteenth of last month.'

'What happened after that?'

'We carried on working as usual. Public cleansing was one of the exceptions.'

'And the epidemic? What was there to see?'

'I heard rumours that thousands and thousands of people were in hospital. That people were dying like flies. And they needed blood donors. And so . . .'

'And so?'

'Well, a week or so after the first announcement, the TV and radio went off the air and we were ordered to stop work. And then we got this other notice. There was no danger any longer, they said, but we were to lay in supplies of food and water and stay at home. And they needed blood donors.'

'Did you volunteer?'

'To give blood? No. I heard of some people who did, but . . .'

'But what?'

'They never came back.'

'Have you been out since then?'

'Oh yes. They only brought in the total curfew a week ago, last Wednesday. The day before that, the water was cut off. The electricity had gone a few days before that, on the Saturday.'

'How did you receive all these communications?'

'Leaflets were delivered.'

'Who delivered them?'

'Soldiers and nursing staff. And then they went round in loudspeaker vans shouting nobody was to go out and blood donors were urgently needed, and to only take orders from doctors and medical professionals.'

'Did the buses go on running?'

'No, no. The buses stopped long before that. At the same time as they gave up publishing the newspapers.'

'How many people are there left here?'

'Don't know. A few.'

'Where are the rest?'

The man gave Jensen a long stare. Eventually he said:

'Don't you know?'

'No. Where are they?'

'I've no idea. No idea at all.'

'When did they move out?'

'They didn't move out,' said the woman. 'They were taken.'

'Taken?'

'It's odd that you don't know. We thought it must be the same all over the city.'

'Were they all taken at the same time?'

'First it was the children. That was the evening before the state of emergency and curfew came in. A bus turned up outside here. I saw it from the window.'

'What sort of bus?'

'An ordinary red, public service bus. There were four of them in it. Two men and two women. They went from door to door and took all the children under twelve. There weren't very many round here.'

'Didn't you open the door?'

'Oh yes. It was the last time we opened the door to anybody. One of the women, it was. She wanted to take him with her.'

The man gestured towards the boy.

'But we refused. Then she got angry and said that if she'd been able to, she'd have taken him from us by force. She even tried it, but I kicked her out.'

'Why did she want the child?'

'She said it was in his own best interests. She said we didn't fully appreciate the situation. She said that if they'd been allowed to, they'd have taken us, too.'

'Who was this woman?'

'Don't know. We'd never seen her before. Some sort of nurse, I think. She didn't say. But she had some kind of uniform on. Green overalls.'

'Where were they going to take the children?'

'To a safe place,' she said. 'When I asked where, she said she didn't know. We didn't dare let him go.'

'What about the others round here?'

'Lots of them went. I saw them putting them on to the bus and driving away.'

'How many children were there?'

'Twenty-five, maybe thirty.'

Jensen did a rapid calculation. That would have been virtually all the children in a district like this.

'Poor parents,' said the woman. 'What monsters, taking the children.'

'And you don't know who these people were?'

'No.'

'Did they have armbands?'

'No, nothing like that.'

'Were any of the children ill?'

'Not as far as I know.'

'And what happened after that?'

'The next day they brought in the curfew. The state of emergency. The children had gone by then.'

'But other than that, people were still here in their flats?'

'Yes, but nobody went out. The next morning, it was the Thursday of last week, three ambulances and four buses came charging in to the car park down there with sirens and the whole works.'

'What kind of buses?'

'Army ones, I think. There were several doctors or healthcare

workers with white coats, and then there must have been a dozen
sanitation soldiers. I recognised the uniforms. I was in the
medical corps when I did my military service.'

'No police?'

'We didn't see any, but we were only peering out of the
window, trying not to be seen. Oh, you asked about armbands.
Well this lot had blue armbands. All of them. A woman doctor
or nurse in a white coat shouted through a megaphone that
everybody who wasn't sick had to be evacuated because of the
epidemic. We were going to a place where there wasn't such
risk of infection. She said we didn't need to take anything with
us, because we'd soon be back and everything we needed would
be provided where we were going. We just had to get down
there quickly, and leave the doors of our flats open so they
could be sprayed with disinfectant. And then we'd be vacci-
nated. She said it was on the orders of some chief or other.'

'The chief medical officer?'

'That's right. Loads of people went down voluntarily and
got on the buses.'

'You didn't?'

'No . . . we'd been petrified ever since what happened to the
children. We stayed here.'

'Did anything else happen?'

The man looked at his wife, not sure how to go on.

'It was horrible,' she said. 'When people stopped coming out,
no matter how much they shouted, the doctors and sanitation
soldiers went up the staircases . . .'

'Go on.'

'I went out on to the landing,' the man said uncertainly. 'And
I . . . well, I heard them at some of the locked doors, and they
smashed them down and hauled out the people who'd stayed

behind. So we opened our front door and hid in the wardrobe. They didn't find us.'

'I had my hand over his mouth the whole time,' said the woman, looking at the boy. 'I was afraid I was going to suffocate him. But then, after about half an hour, we heard the sirens again and the motor engine noise as they drove off. Then we thought it would be safe to come out.'

'And nobody's been here since then?'

'Not until you came,' said the man. 'But ambulances drive past every so often. They collect up anyone they find outside and take them away.'

'We mustn't go out,' said the woman, squeezing the child's hand.

'Is it just you in this block now?'

The man and woman exchanged doubtful glances.

'Did you hear the question?' said Jensen.

'Yes,' said the man, 'I heard.'

'Well?'

'No, there are some others here. They must have done the same as us. Hidden. We never see them, but we hear them.'

'The sound really carries here,' the woman said apologetically.

Jensen still had his eyes fixed on the man.

'One more thing,' he said.

'Yes?'

'Why didn't you obey the evacuation order when so many other people did? And why didn't you let the child be taken to a place of safety?'

The man shifted his weight to the other foot and looked round nervously.

'Answer the question.'

'Well, I went on working longer than most people, and . . .'

'And?'

'Er, I knew the blokes at work who were on the trains and trucks that collected the rubbish from the main hospital and that big detoxification unit. They said . . .'

He stopped.

'What did they say?'

'That anyone who went into hospital caught it and died. Blood donors and anybody else.'

'But your colleagues didn't catch it?'

'No, they were never let into the actual buildings.'

'So it was all just rumour?'

'Yes,' the man said.

Jensen studied his notebook for a while. Then he said:

'What had happened earlier. Before the epidemic?'

They looked at him, confused.

'Nothing,' said the man. 'I was working.'

'There were disturbances. The election was postponed, wasn't it?'

'So I heard. But we didn't see anything about it on TV or in the papers.'

'Nothing at all?'

'Only that they were putting off the election because there were antisocial elements trying to sabotage it.'

'Were there any of these antisocial elements at your own place of work?'

The man shrugged.

'Well, I don't really know. The police came for a few people.'

'What sort of police?'

'Don't know. But someone said they were the secret police.'

'There's no such thing as the secret police.'

'Oh. Isn't there?'

'No. How many were arrested?'

'Only a handful. And a few others made themselves scarce.'

'Where did they go?'

'I don't know.'

'Are you interested in politics yourself?'

'No.'

'Do you usually vote?'

'For the Accord? Yes, of course.'

The woman shifted uneasily.

'That's not true,' she said quietly.

The man gave her a miserable look.

'If I'm being honest, we don't bother these days. But that's not a crime, is it?'

'No.'

The man gave a shrug.

'Why vote?' he said. 'It's all beyond us, anyway.'

Jensen closed his notebook.

'So you didn't witness any of these disturbances yourself?'

'No. I only heard rumours.'

'What sort of rumours?'

'That lots of people got so incensed with the socialists that they beat them up.'

'When?'

'At demos and so on. But I expect they only got what they deserved.'

Jensen put away his notebook and pen.

'Do you know who smashed the window of the supermarket down there?'

'Yes, it was the same lot as came for the children. They broke into the shop and took loads of stuff out to the bus. Stuff they sold in the shop, I mean.'

The boy said something incomprehensible. The woman tried to shush him.

'What's he saying?' asked Jensen.

'He's asking if Mister Policeman's got a bang-bang,' she said, blushing. 'He means a gun.'

'No, I haven't got a gun.'

Jensen looked at the open bag of sweets in the child's hand and said:

'Don't forget to pay for that when things get back to normal again.'

The man nodded.

'Or there could be unpleasant consequences.'

Jensen moved towards the door. The woman went after him and said, quiet and hesitantly:

'When will things get back to normal?'

'Don't know. You'll be safest indoors until further notice. Goodbye.'

No one in the flat said anything more.

Inspector Jensen left. He closed the door carefully behind him.

CHAPTER 15

There was not much to see on the way to the Sixteenth District police station. The streets of the inner city lay empty and the whole city centre looked completely deserted. All the shops were locked and barred, as were the snack bars where the private food industry syndicates that had won contracts from the Ministry of Public Health used to serve up their scientifically composed but far from tempting set meals. The only sign of any kind of care and loving attention to detail were the names of these food outlets. They were invariably called 'Culinary Paradise', with subheadings such as 'The Dainty Morsel', 'Chef's Delight' or 'Eats and Treats'. The windows displayed fake, plastic food, and alongside them and inside the premises there were notices distributed jointly by the Ministry for Public Health and the group of companies that ran the restaurants. Most of these said 'Chew your food well, but do not occupy your table for too long. Other citizens are waiting.' This concise message encapsulated the primary interests of both parties. During his long period of illness Jensen had had problems with his digestion, and had only patronised such places on rare occasions. He knew, however, that the food was cooked centrally and sent out pre-portioned. A few years before, the operation had been rationalised so that all the outlets in the city served only a single daily dish, a move that had generated significant savings, that is to say, greatly improved profitability, for the conglomerate producing the food. The standard dishes were allegedly geared to popular taste and were devised by a group of experts inside the Ministry of Public Health. A typical dish might consist of three slices of meat loaf, two baked onions, five mushy boiled potatoes, a lettuce leaf, half a tomato, some thick, flour-based sauce, a third of a litre of homogenised milk, three slices of bread or crispbread, a portion of vitamin-enriched margarine, a little tub of soft cheese, coffee in a plastic cup, and a cake. The next day it would be the same thing again, but with boiled fish instead of the meat. The whole lot was served on hygienically packed plastic trays, covered in plastic film. The profit motive had dictated that almost all the private companies in the business had gradually been sucked up by the big food industry conglomerates.

Those who made a study of solidarity issues had long since discovered that when hundreds of thousands of people ate exactly the same food at exactly the same time, the result was an enhanced sense of security and a collective sense of belonging. The bosses of this socially useful production chain were not resident in the country. They had been living on islands in more southerly climes for many years. There were regular features on them in the weekly magazines. These would have pictures of them relaxing on yachts or standing by white marble balustrades with palm trees and surf-fringed beaches in the background.

The streets were dotted with carelessly parked cars, and there were military vehicles abandoned at some of the major crossroads, just as at the airport. Most of them were tanks or armoured cars. In some places, windows had been smashed and walls bore bullet marks, but there was no evidence anywhere of direct destruction or serious damage. Jensen saw no living people, and no dead bodies. Nor did he come across any ambulances or other motor vehicles, but as he negotiated the maze of intersections at the city hall, he saw a column of trucks moving along highway seven. They had full loads on the back, covered with tarpaulins, and to judge by their direction of travel they were heading for the central detoxification unit. The convoy had no escort.

Fifteen minutes later he was at the Sixteenth District station. He turned through the arch and saw his own police car parked in the usual place, though not as neatly as he would have done it himself. On checking he found that the doors were not locked and the key was in the ignition. Inspector Jensen gave a slight shake of the head. He had always thought the head of the plainclothes patrol slipshod and imprecise in his actions. His reports left a good deal to be desired, as they were often unfocused and cluttered with irrelevant detail. He would never contemplate recommending the man for a position of higher command.

The doors to the police station were also unlocked. The large reception area with its old-fashioned decor and fittings was deserted, and there was nothing to indicate any human presence, living or dead, in the station as a whole. He looked about him, and then went calmly up the spiral staircase to his office, hung up his outdoor things, and sat down at his desk for the first time in three months. Glanced at the electric wall clock. It had stopped, for the first time in fifteen years.

The untidiness of the desk was plain to see, and it annoyed him. Pens, pencils and sheets of paper were lying all over the place. He opened a drawer and found the same thing there. It took him a good quarter of an hour to restore order around him. Then he went to the filing cabinet, took out the log that was supposed to be kept by the duty district inspector, opened the large, paper-bound volume in front of him on the desk and began to study it. He went back to his own last day on duty and read the final entry, signed by himself.

Handed over command, 10.00.

Further down the same page, his successor had written:

Have arrested 39 of the 43 on list I was given. Plainclothes from some security service came to get them for questioning. Jensen seems to have messed up somehow, but then he was ill.

The entry was typical of the man's inability to express himself. Jensen wrinkled his nose, not at the impertinence of the comment but at the clumsy, unclear way it was worded.

He read on. The entries for the first week were merely numbers of drunks apprehended and sudden death incidents. For example:

48 alcohol abuse cases this evening. Two killed themselves.

Then the man had clearly realised this was an unfortunate choice of words, crossed out 'killed themselves' and wrote 'died suddenly in the cells' instead.

A few days later:

Still haven't been sent a new doctor. Difficult.

Jensen glanced through a few more pages and found the following entirely misplaced comment:

New doctor came today. Heard Jensen's as good as dead and going to be cremated over there. No point bringing the body home, says the head of personnel at HQ. The lads here are collecting for a decent, realistic-looking plastic wreath.

On the twenty-first of September, a Saturday, there was an entry completely out of keeping with the rest.

Whole force out to protect a demonstration march from agitated civilians. Went fine, but mood very heated.

And a week later:

More demo trouble. Much worse than last time, but we more or less coped. Manpower from lots of districts involved. Aggravating for police officers, forced to take the demonstrators' part against nice, law-abiding citizens.

On the third of September his stand-in had written:

Major riot at political demo. Backup called in from outlying districts.

A week later:

Total chaos and running battles at the party offices and outside friendly embassies. Tough for the police. Lots of them acting against their own convictions.

And a few days after that:

We've finally been ordered to carry weapons and go in hard.

The entry for the twenty-first of October was particularly sloppily written and inadequately formulated:

The elections have been postponed and there's no order any more. The socialists dare not attack the friendly embassies now. The loyal part of the population has had enough and is besieging the embassy buildings of powers hostile to the people. We can't protect them, and nobody in the force wants to anyway. Have heard the diplomats are closing their offices and getting out.

Jensen read on.

Only two drunks last night. No time for them any more.

Long arrest list from the secret branch. 125 names. Got hold of 86. The rest must be in hiding.

Another arrest list from the secret services. Tried to get hold of the police chief today. He's out of the country. Most of the government, too. Hard to get proper orders.

This last entry had been written on the thirtieth of October. The next day came the following summary:

Military assistance deployed this morning. Tanks, armoured cars, all sorts. Have been notified that the traitors of the nation are planning a major coup on Saturday, it's in the papers and it's been on radio and TV. Police morale is better than ever. They're all itching to put the socialists in their place, once and for all.

There was also an entirely superfluous addition:

Shame old J. wasn't here for this. Hope he's having a nice time up there in heaven!

Jensen read the unorthodox sentences with a frown of displeasure. Moved on to the critical Saturday:

Almost all the red scum crushed by us and the army. Lots of law-abiding citizens helping out. What a day!

Two days later:

Three bloody socialists came here today and asked for protection! Got what they deserved.

A comment on the twelfth of November hinted at flagging enthusiasm:

Everything seems normal again. The military are still here, but we can get back to the drunks.

But the entry for the very next day sounded the alarm.

Some epidemic has broken out. Our cars commandeered as ambulances.

Confirmation came on the fifteenth of November:

Extremely contagious illness. Already thirty per cent absence in this district. Health officials seriously concerned.

Then there were no entries for a week.

More than fifty per cent of staff off sick, a lot have died. All cars that can be manned are taking the sick and dead to the national detox centre and blood donors to the main hospital.

And three days later:

The illness is extremely catching. Not feeling so good myself. Short of staff, despite army help.

There were only three further entries. They were unsigned and in different handwriting.

Monday 25 Nov. Acting Inspector died yesterday. Cremated immediately.

Wednesday 27 Nov. State of emergency.

Saturday 30 Nov. All police and army officers fit for duty now to take orders from the medical authorities. About to report to the chief medical officer.

The note was four days old, and it was the last in the diary.

Inspector Jensen read everything through again. Then he got out his ballpoint pen and wrote neatly:

Wednesday 4 Dec. Resumed command 10.30. Station unmanned. J–n.

He closed the diary and returned it to its place.

Back at his desk, he thought he heard a faint sound in the building, presumably from the cells.

CHAPTER 16

Inspector Jensen went down the spiral staircase and across the deserted reception area, opened a steel door and made his way to the basement. In the newly built cell block, the ceiling and floor were painted white and the cells had bars of shiny steel. Despite the overcast weather and the lack of artificial light, it was not as dark down there as one might have expected. The vast majority of the cells were empty and standing open. Two of the doors, however, were shut and locked. He looked through the bars into the first of them. On the bunk below the high, barred window lay a woman. She was naked and her clothes were strewn around the cell floor. She was lying on her back and he knew at a glance that she was dead, and had in all likelihood been so for several days. Her flesh was chalk-white and her eyes wide open. She was quite young, and the usual type, blonde and smooth-skinned, her armpits and pubic area shaved. Apart from the unnatural pallor, death had not altered her appearance to any marked degree. The chill of the unheated basement had evidently helped to preserve the body. Jensen did not bother to unlock the door to scrutinise her at closer hand. Instead he moved on to the other locked cell. It was on the left, at the far end of the corridor. Here, too, there was someone stretched out on the bunk. But this time it was a man and what was more, he was alive. He was lying with his face to the wall, and had cocooned himself in the grey police blanket. Seemed to be shaking with cold. The cell stank of urine and excrement. Jensen stood there watching him for a few moments. Then he got out his key ring, unlocked the door and went in. The man turned his head and stared at him. His face was hollow, his eyes bloodshot and crusted. Grizzled stubble on his chin, sunken cheeks.

'What,' he said hoarsely. 'Who . . .'

'How long have you been here?' asked Jensen.

'Four or five days,' the man said in a weak voice. 'Roughly.'

'Why were you arrested?'

'The usual. Booze.'

Jensen nodded.

'I've been in three times already.'

Three drinking offences meant immediate transfer to a rehabilitation centre for alcoholics, or detox clinic as it was known nowadays. This was routine procedure.

'But no bus showed up to fetch me the next morning. Nobody showed up at all. If I hadn't had the bowl of washing water I'd have died of thirst.'

'Have you been here alone all this time?'

'The pigs . . . sorry . . . the police brought in a girl at the same time as me. Are you a policeman?'

'Yes.'

'But I don't think she was drunk. Or that wasn't the only thing, at any rate. I only saw her for a few seconds when they were searching us. But I heard her. Shrieking and howling and shouting all sorts of weird stuff. I haven't heard her for the last couple of days.'

Jensen nodded again. Looked at the man and said:

'Can you walk all right?'

'I think so. I haven't had anything to eat since I got here. Only that bloody washing water.'

'Come with me.'

The arrested man struggled free of the blanket and got slowly and unsteadily to his feet. Jensen took him by the arm and led him up to reception. The man was haggard and in poor physical condition, presumably as a result of advanced alcoholism rather than the starvation cure he had endured in the last few days.

In the canteen next to the reception area, Jensen found a few packets of biscuits and a bag of rusks. He also took with him three bottles of fizzy drink and the two identity cards he found in the card index system where the IDs of those under arrest were kept overnight.

He took the man up to his office, and while the latter cautiously nibbled his way through a few biscuits and gulped down one of the fizzy drinks, he carefully studied the two identity cards.

The woman had been twenty-six and unmarried. Her profession was given as computer operator in the Department of Communications. She had never been arrested for drunkenness, and had not been this time, either. The charge was offending public decency.

The man was forty-seven and described as a casual labourer. He had already had three spells in the alcohol clinic and the three red marks on his card showed that he was indeed due for a fourth period of treatment. The length of the treatment was increased by a month each time. You started with a month, then went on to two, three, four and so on. After five stays in the institution, you were considered beyond human help and interned for an indefinite period. That was the routine procedure.

Jensen observed the man, who was now eating with rather

greater enthusiasm. When the first packet of biscuits was gone, the arrested man said dubiously:

'I wonder . . .'

'Yes?'

'You wouldn't happen to have a drop of the hard stuff?'

There was a locked room in the police station where relatively large amounts of alcoholic drink, confiscated from those taken under arrest, were stored to await quarterly collection by the lorries of the state alcohol monopoly for resale to customers.

'It's against the rules to consume alcohol here,' Jensen said unsympathetically.

'I see. It's just that I'm freezing cold.'

Jensen got out his notebook.

'I'm going to ask you a few questions,' he said.

'Fire away.'

'You said that woman didn't seem drunk. On what basis do you make that assertion?'

'Well, I only heard her, as I say. She was bellowing and screaming. I think she was sick, or crazy.'

'Could you hear what she was saying?'

'Yes, sometimes. She shouted that everything was red, that there was a red fog in her cell.'

'Go on.'

'She yelled obscenities.'

'What sort of obscenities?'

'All sorts. She shouted something about not being able to bear having clothes on. Said she was free and couldn't restrain her body. And loads of other stuff. Then she cried and howled, like an animal. But I haven't heard her for a couple of days now. Maybe even three. I'm not very sure.'

'What were the circumstances of your arrest?'

'It was stupid. Avoidable.'

'In what way?'

'I was plastered, of course. Had been for weeks. But then I tripped over down there on the front steps and fell asleep.'

'The front steps here?'

'Yes. Or at least, that's where I was lying when a pig . . . when a policeman in uniform woke me up and brought me in.'

'Who searched you?'

'The same bloke. The one who woke me up. He was the only one I saw. I thought the bus would be coming in the morning to take me to the dryer, but nobody came back. Not until just now, when you turned up and let me out.'

'When did you first see the woman?'

'The policeman who nabbed me had her with him.'

'Why?'

'I don't know. I don't think she'd been drinking.'

'So you said.'

'I think she was out of her mind. She screamed and hurled insults and told the policeman to fucking well leave her alone and concentrate on rooting out the vermin instead.'

'What vermin?'

'I don't know. Then she pulled up her dress and showed . . . well, her cunt.'

'How did the police officer behave?'

'Oh, he was nice enough. Stayed calm. Said that he had a lot to do. That he'd arrange for me to be picked up and taken to the dryer. And he said he'd send a doctor down to take a look at that girl. But nobody ever came. I don't think so, anyway. He had to go to the hospital, he said. He'd be back soon. But

he didn't come. Nobody came. If I hadn't had that washbowl
. . . are you sure you haven't got anything to drink?'

Jensen did not reply.

'It's so cold,' said the alcoholic. 'I'm freezing.'

'I'll make sure you've got some food supplies and extra
blankets. One more thing.'

'What's that?'

'How were things before this happened?'

'Great.'

'What do you mean by great?'

'Just what I say. Things have never been so good as these
past couple of months.'

'In what way?'

'In every way. You've gathered I drink a lot. I was a car
mechanic before. I haven't got anywhere proper to live, have
to find places here and there. And always running scared of
the cops. Trying to keep out of the way so as not to get nailed
again and sent to dry out.'

The man sat grumbling to himself for a minute or two. Then
he said:

'I'm in for four months this time.'

'So what was it that was so great?'

'Suddenly nobody cared about us alkies. The police couldn't
give a damn about us. Said they had too much else on. Spent
every day having a go at people carrying placards and that.
Some political hullabaloo. Loads of soldiers, too. Firing shots
and carrying on.'

'And the elections were postponed?'

'What elections?'

'The government elections. The democratic elections.'

'Oh, them. They're nothing to do with ordinary people. I

never vote. Politics is only for a few types who understand what it's all about. Making the decisions and that. Well, and then . . .'

'Yes.'

'All of a sudden, nobody had to work any more. Some catching disease started spreading. People died of it, they said.'

'Aren't you afraid of this disease?'

'Pah, everyone's got to die of something or other in the end.'

'So you don't know what's been happening?'

'Nope, haven't the foggiest. There were fewer and fewer people about and the street lamps went out. I was drunk most of the time, of course. Pity I had to go and collapse in a heap on the steps of a police station.'

'Can you read?'

'You bet I can. We learnt at school. But . . .'

'But what?'

'I never read anything, of course. It's only ever things for other people. Stuff that makes no sense.' They sat in silence for a while. Then the man said:

'Is it over now, that disease?'

'I don't think so.'

'Ah.'

'According to the note on your identity card, you've been here five days and nights. Did you see or hear anything in that time? Apart from the woman in cell eight?'

The man thought.

'Well, yes. Yesterday.'

'Who was it?'

'I didn't see anybody. But I heard a car come into the yard. Heard the engine. It sounded like a jeep. I was a mechanic before . . . well, before I got like this. I can recognise engines by the sound. A jeep, I think.'

'What then?'

'Somebody got out. Only one person. You could tell from the footsteps. He didn't come down to the cells. It sounded as though he was going up into the main building.'

'He? Are you sure it was a man?'

'Sounded like it.'

'And then?'

'I tried calling out, but my voice was all croaky, and after a while he drove off again.'

'Anything else?'

'No.'

Jensen closed his notepad and put down his pen. Collected up the rusks, fizzy drink bottles and the rest of the biscuits. Took the man back down to the arrest suite, fetched blankets, a slop bucket and a can of water and put him in a clean cell. Locked him in.

'Are you certain you wouldn't like to give me a drop of booze?' the man said.

'Yes, I'm certain. I shall make sure you're taken to the rehabilitation centre as soon as possible.'

He returned to his office, sat down at the desk and read slowly through all the notes he had made. After about an hour he heard the sound of a vehicle engine, rose and went to the window.

A small jeep with a canvas top turned in through the gateway. It parked so close to the wall that Jensen could not see who was getting out.

CHAPTER 17

Inspector Jensen sat at his office desk, listening.

Whoever had got out of the jeep made no effort to move cautiously or conceal what they were doing. Footsteps echoed across the ground-floor reception area and then up the spiral staircase. The visitor was already in the corridor, passing Jensen's room. To judge by the steps and the breathing, the person in question was carrying something heavy. A door opened and shut. As far as Jensen could tell, the person had gone into the radio control room.

He left it a couple of minutes. In the meantime, he thought he could make out faint, mechanical sounds.

Jensen stood up, left the room and walked the few steps to the radio control room. Knocked lightly on the door before he opened it.

There was a man bending over the radio control console. Beside him on the floor were two accumulators in wooden boxes. They looked like extra-large car batteries. The man turned and stared towards the door. Jensen recognised him at once. The red-haired police doctor.

The man was wearing a boiler suit of green khaki and rubber boots and had a sub-machine gun on a strap over his left shoulder, its muzzle pointing down at the floor.

'Ah,' he said slowly. 'Jensen. I was just wondering where the car in the yard had come from. It wasn't there yesterday. You pulled through, then?'

'Yes. What are you doing?'

'I thought I'd try to get this contraption going,' the doctor said, unconcerned. 'What are you up to yourself?'

'I'm trying to find out what really happened.'

'That's not easy.'

The police doctor shook his head thoughtfully and turned back to the radio equipment.

'So you pulled through,' he said again. 'I didn't expect you to. When did you get back?'

Jensen checked the time.

'An hour ago.'

'And now you're trying to find out what's happened?'

'Yes. And what's still happening.'

The doctor shook his head again.

'It won't be easy,' he said. 'How did you get into the country?'

'By helicopter.'

'Sent by the government?'

'More or less.'

After a pause, Jensen asked:

'Do you know what's happened?'

'Parts of it.'

'What, then?'

'Something terrible.'

'I've already worked out that much.'

'Unfortunately also something that's a completely logical consequence. It's a long story. Very long.'

'Tell me.'

'I haven't got time right now. And anyway, you know almost as much as I do. If you give yourself time to think it through.'

'I've been away for over three months.'

'True enough. Quite a bit has happened in that time. But all the essentials happened before you left. Long before.'

He busied himself with his flexes and contacts for a while. Looked up and said:

'Do you know your way around this stuff?'

'No.'

'We'll just have to do the best we can, then.'

There was a crackle from the equipment. A voice crystallised out of the rush of the ether.

'Vehicle twenty-seven here. Can you hear us?'

'Of course I can. What is it?'

Jensen recognised both the voice and the lazy drawl. The woman who had been speaking to the men in the white coats.

'The main hospital is in contact with an ambulance,' he said.

'You should have shot them.'

'I'm not armed. And anyway, they showed their ID.'

'You should still have killed them.'

The police doctor turned down the radio conversation. Looked quizzically at Jensen.

'How much do you actually know?' he said at length.

'Very little.'

'I don't know everything either. I didn't get back until yesterday. To the city, I mean. There are things I don't understand any more than you do.'

'Where were you before that?'

'Out in the country. In the forest.'

'Were you in hiding?'

'Yes.'

'You were arrested, weren't you?'

The police doctor gave him a long look.

'No, I wasn't arrested.'

Jensen said nothing.

'Thanks to you,' said the doctor.

'You mean you escaped?'

'Yes. I never went down those stairs. I stopped outside the door and heard you ring the duty officer. So I went up to the roof and scrambled over to the building next door. I ran away.'

'Then I ought to arrest you.'

The police doctor shook his head.

'There are no police any more. Only you. As far as I know. And as far as I know, there's no government to give you orders, either. Or me, for that matter. No one who can order us to behave like idiots any longer.'

'I don't understand what you mean.'

The man flicked a switch on the control console.

'There we are,' he said. 'This is working now, anyway. We might need it later on.'

'You're talking in riddles,' said Jensen.

'Yes. And what's more, I haven't time for it. Every ten minutes, someone dies. Needlessly. And not far from here.'

'The epidemic?'

The police doctor nodded. He went towards the door. Stopped and turned round. His eyes were bloodshot, he was in need of a shave and looked very tired.

'Jensen?'

'Yes.'

'Are you in touch with your . . . the people who sent you on this mission?'

'No.'

'Are you interested in politics?'

'No.'

'Do you know anything about politics?'

'No more than most people.'

'Good. I want you to help me with something.'

'What's that?'

'I've got someone down there in the car. A man. He's in a pretty bad way. It would be useful if you could look after him until I get back. Come on.'

Jensen nodded and went down to the jeep with him.

'Help me carry him,' said the police doctor. 'There's a sofa in the room next to yours, isn't there?'

'Yes there is.'

'Let's put him there.'

The man looked thirty or so. He was lying on the back seat of the jeep, wrapped in a blanket. His skin was pallid and his cheeks were hollow. There was nothing to indicate he was conscious. As they carried him up the spiral staircase, he felt very light. When they had put him down on the sofa, the doctor threw back the blanket and Jensen saw that the man was disabled. Both legs were missing below the knee.

'Shouldn't this man be in hospital?'

'He's just come from there,' said the doctor.

Jensen looked at him enquiringly.

'He's asleep now, but he'll wake up soon. I gave him an injection. When he perks up, you can talk to him. I'm sure there's plenty he can tell you. Mentally there's nothing wrong with him.'

The doctor shrugged.

'Strangely enough,' he said.

'You can interview him,' he added in a sarcastic tone.

'Who is he?'

'A good friend. If he's in pain, give him one of these tablets. They put him to sleep for an hour. But the pain goes. He may need to take them at pretty frequent intervals. And make sure he gets something to drink, if there is anything. If you have to go out, leave the tablets where he can reach them and give him something to read.'

'But what if anybody comes?'

'Nobody's going to come here. There isn't anyone in the city centre. Yet. Are you going to carry on with your so-called investigation?'

Jensen nodded.

'In that case I've got a tip-off for you. The Steel Spring.'

'The Steel Spring.'

'Yes. Find out what it means. You can always ask somebody. You could try the Ministry of the Interior or the secret police. Or the party offices.'

'There's no such thing as the secret police.'

'No. You're right. But there used to be. I've got to go now.'

He looked at his watch.

'I'll be back this evening, by about seven.'

'One more thing,' said Jensen.

'What?'

'There's a dead woman in one of the cells. You should take a look at her.'

'Perhaps I should.'

They went down to the arrest suite. The alcoholic had dozed off on his bunk but was shaking under his blankets.

'Who's that poor devil?' said the police doctor.

'Alcoholic, third-timer.'

'Why don't you give him a bottle from the confiscation store?'

'It's against regulations.'

'There are no regulations any more, Jensen. And this man's freezing.'

They moved on to the cell where the dead woman was, opened

the steel-barred door and went in. The police doctor gave her a cursory look and ran the tip of his index finger along the skin of her stomach.

'The epidemic?' Jensen asked curiously.

'Yes. The illness. She died of it. Look how the skin's almost transparent. The genitals unnaturally swollen.'

'What's the illness called?'

'I don't know.'

He paused and then said:

'It's a new invention.'

'Is there a cure?'

'No. If you'd taken a blood sample from her just before she died, it would have looked like cream.'

'Is there a vaccine?'

'No.'

'Aren't you afraid of catching it?'

'No.'

The police doctor looked gravely at Jensen.

'This illness isn't infectious,' he said.

CHAPTER 18

The man on the sofa shifted uneasily and opened his eyes. Thirty-five minutes had elapsed since the police doctor had climbed into the jeep and driven off. Jensen pulled his chair up closer and caught the man's uncomprehending eye.

'You're at the main station in the Sixteenth District. My name's Jensen.'

He made a move to get his ID badge from his breast pocket, but stopped himself and let his hand fall back. Instead he said:

'Do you want something to drink?'

The invalid nodded, moistening his lips with his tongue.

'Yes please.'

His voice was clear and youthful.

'Your friend brought you here. He'll be back later. Are you in pain?'

The man shook his head. Jensen opened one of the bottles of fizzy drink and poured it into a plastic cup. The man took it and drank. His hands shook.

'Have you always been disabled?'

'What? Oh, that. No, not at all.'

'How long?'

'I don't really know. What day is it? Today, I mean.'

'Wednesday the fourth of December.'

'Oh, I see. It's cold here.'

Jensen went for another blanket. Spread it over the man.

'Does that feel any better?'

'Yes, thanks. What was it you were asking?'

'What have you been through?'

'It's a long story. You know what's happened as well as I do.'

'No.'

The invalid gave him a curious look and said:

'Who are you, anyway?'

Jensen took out his service badge.

'Police. Inspector Jensen. Sixteenth District.'

'I hate the police.'

'Why's that?'

'How can someone like you ask that? What are you planning to do with me?'

'Nothing. Look after you until your friend comes back.'

The man on the sofa seemed as confused as ever.

'Fourth of December,' he said to himself. 'So it's been more than a month.'

'Since what?'

'Since the second of November.'

'What happened on the second of November?'

'Don't you remember? Are you mad?'

'I wasn't here. I didn't come until the day before yesterday.'

'I don't believe you. You're trying to trick me.'

The man turned his head away, lay with his face to the back of the sofa.

'What am I trying to trick you into?' asked Jensen.

The other man gave no reply and Jensen did not repeat his question. Outside, the rain had turned to snow. Big, wet snowflakes plastered themselves against the windowpanes. At length, the man on the sofa said:

'You're right, of course. What could you trick me into?'

Renewed silence.

'What do you want to know?'

'I'm trying to find out what's happened.'

'I can only say what happened to me personally.'

After a brief pause he added:

'And to some people I know.'

Jensen was silent for a while. Then he said:

'You know the police doctor for the Sixteenth District, for example.'

'Yes.'

'Have you known him long?'

'For some years, yes. Five or six at least.'

'How did you get to know him?'

'We were members of the same club. Or society, if you like.'

'What sort of society?'

'A district political society.'

'A communist league?'

'More like socialist. At least that's what we called it.'

The man turned his head.

'It's not illegal,' he said suddenly. 'Political clubs aren't illegal.'

'No.'

'Demonstrating isn't illegal either.'

'Not at all. Who said it was?'

'Nobody. But still . . .'

He broke off and looked Jensen in the eye.

'Is it true you weren't here on the second of November?'

'Yes. It's true. What did you do in your political society?'

'We discussed various issues.'

'And what conclusion did you reach?'

'That prevailing social practices were and are to be condemned. That the whole thing needed to be torn up.'

'Why?'

'Because the so-called Accord has never been anything but a bluff. It came into being because the old, supposedly socialist movement was losing its hold on employees and the working classes. And at that moment, the social democrats sold their voters lock, stock and barrel to the right wing. They entered into the grand coalition, or Accord as it later came to be known, just because a handful of people wanted to cling to power. They abandoned socialism, made successive changes to their party programme, and delivered the whole country up to imperialism and the formation of private capital.'

'You can hardly remember all that,' Jensen said indulgently. 'How old are you?'

'Thirty. But I've studied these questions long and hard. To stop the country turning socialist, the social democratic party and the trade union movement deserted their most fundamental ideological principles. The leaders at the time had been in power for so long that they couldn't imagine losing it. What's more, they had discovered that even the labour movement and its mouthpieces could be run on a bourgeois-plutocratic model, with an eye to financial profitability for the few. The Accord's most deeply held principle was that everything had to make a profit. That was why this phantom political combination was entered into and its true nature hidden behind a hypocritical façade of clichés about higher living standards, mutual understanding and security. That everything was getting better all the time.'

'Things did get better,' said Jensen.

'Yes, in material terms, for a while. The individual was physically nannied but intellectually and spiritually neutered. Politics and society became something abstract, of no concern to the individual. And to lure people into all this, they showered them with carefully censored crap in the papers, and on the radio and TV. Until they had almost an entire nation of sheep, until people only knew they had a car and a flat and a TV set and were unhappy. Knew it was more tempting to commit suicide or drink themselves to death than to go to work.'

'Do you feel like a sheep?'

'I said almost. There were groups of politically active individuals, and once the low-water mark was reached, they started to grow again. More and more people realised that what the so-called theorists of the Accord philosophy called standard of living and peaceful revolution was nothing other than a criminal attempt to make people accept the universal meaninglessness that had resulted from a crazed political and sociological experiment. It's amazing it took so long for everyone to see it. All you had to do was look about you. It was meaningless to work, meaningless to learn anything except a few technical operations. Even the physical aspects of life became meaningless: eating, sex, having children.'

'You didn't come up with all that by yourself,' said Jensen.

'No, I didn't. I'm mainly quoting what others have said and written. But I understand it well enough to see how bad things are.'

'If we can stick to the facts for a moment,' said Jensen. 'What else did you do in your political club? Did you organise demonstrations?'

'Yes.'

'And what did you hope to gain by them?'

'We were working to make people understand their own situation. To crush Accord society. It was only once we'd blown the Accord apart that we could get at our arch-enemies.'

'Which arch-enemies?'

'Well, social democracy, which had betrayed the labour movement and sold out to capitalism. And then the capitalist system as a whole.'

'And how were you able to do it?'

'There weren't all that many of us, but on the other hand, numbers kept growing. At first the police were the only ones who took any notice of the demonstrations. The vast mass was entirely indifferent to them, as expected. People had been rendered entirely apathetic by the attempt to impose standardisation on them by all available means. Gradually even the police stopped opposing us, on the orders of the government I assume. We interpreted it . . .'

'Yes? How did you interpret it?'

'We interpreted it as a positive development. We thought that the people pulling the strings had taken fright and wanted to avoid drawing attention to our actions at any cost. They succeeded to the extent that the vast majority of people still didn't take any notice of us, although our numbers were swelling and we demonstrated more and more often. The only thing that seemed to annoy people was our obstructing the traffic. But the police soon started helping us with that, too, and directed the protest marches to their destinations as smoothly as they could. We saw that as a sign of fear, too. Of the regime seeing its main role, as usual, as that of not distressing people, not waking them up from their dream world of material affluence and strictly contained anxiety.'

'Did your organisations make any headway in elections?'

'In a way.'

'What do you mean?'

'Well we didn't get all that many votes, but more and more people abstained from voting. Even that, the fact that political ignorance was growing at the same rate as boredom and suppressed dissatisfaction, showed us that we were right. Of those who did take part in the elections, almost all of them voted for the Accord, of course.'

'Why?'

'From sheer force of habit. They or their parents had once upon a time learnt to vote either for social democracy or for the right-wing parties. And we had no propaganda resources to call on, either. But we carried on campaigning even though our shouts fell on deaf ears, right up until . . .'

'Right up until?'

'Right up until everything changed.'

'And when was that?'

'Some time in September.'

'What changed?'

'I don't know. The people, maybe . . . The first time I noticed anything was on the twenty-first of September.'

'What happened on the twenty-first of September?'

'I'll try to tell you.'

He screwed up his eyes and grimaced with pain.

'Is it hurting?'

'Yes, there's this pain in my legs.'

The man on the sofa writhed convulsively. Groaned.

Jensen took the tube the police doctor had given him, shook out one of the white tablets and poured out another fizzy drink.

'Take this,' he said.

Jensen slid his right hand under the back of the man's neck to raise his head gently so he could swallow the pill.

He suddenly thought of the nurse and the fact that he had once seen her cry.

Within a couple of minutes, the man on the sofa was asleep.

Inspector Jensen sat motionless, watching him calmly and without expression.

CHAPTER 19

Exactly one hour and ten minutes had passed when the man on the sofa woke up again. He opened his eyes and looked at Jensen in bewilderment. After a minute or so, his face cleared.

'Oh yes,' he said. 'Now it comes back to me.'

'Is the pain still bad?'

'No, it's all right now. Thanks.'

The words came huskily, as if the man's throat was dry. Jensen poured a little fruit soda into the plastic cup and supported the man's head. He drained the cup thirstily.

'We were talking about your political activities.'

'Yes, I remember.'

'You explained where you stood.'

'You do understand that we're right?'

'No, but I'd be interested to hear what comes next.'

'There's no more to tell.'

'What happened in September?'

'Oh yes. That.'

The man lay in silence for a few moments. Then, without taking his eyes off Jensen, he said:

'I can't explain what happened. I don't understand it.'

'But you know what happened to you personally.'

'I know what happened to several of us.'

He broke off again.

'But I can't explain it,' he said.

'Let's just stick to the facts,' Jensen said amiably. 'Plain and simple facts.'

'Facts. There are no plain and simple facts.'

'What your job is, for example.'

'I'm a sociologist. Used to work at the alcohol research unit.'

'Was it complicated work?'

'Yes, very complicated.'

'Taxing?'

'Not physically taxing. I was just one of many in the statistics section. We collated figures that came in from the alcohol retailers, the police and the detox clinics. It was easy work in itself.'

'A lot of responsibility?'

'Hardly. Our statistical tables were sent on to higher authorities, where they were worked over. That's to say, they were put through the mill over and over again and sent from one authority to another. When they finally got to, well, whoever they were meant for, they were distorted beyond all recognition. Improved, if you like. Even we, the ones who'd put them together in the first place, had no chance of recognising them.'

He shook his head.

'No, it was a simple job.'

'So what was the difficulty? The complicated part?'

'The difficulties were of an ethical nature.'

'Ethical?'

'Yes. First and foremost, the fact that the whole procedure went against the basic principles of statistical science. The figures we got in were works of fiction from the very start. Then they were further falsified, quite consciously and almost entirely openly. Knowing that made it hard to endure it there.'

'Did your colleagues share your way of seeing it?'

'A few of them did. Most just got on with the job, like robots, without thinking or asking questions. In other words, their attitude to their work was the same as almost everyone else's in this country.'

The man paused for a moment before going on.

'But the really unbearable thing was having to deal with the issue per se.'

He looked at Jensen.

'As a policeman, you've doubtless had plenty of dealings with the alcohol legislation and the way it's applied?' Jensen nodded.

'Drink-driving laws? Being drunk in public places? Domestic alcohol abuse? All that stuff.'

'Yes.'

'Each law more insane than the last one? The number of suicides, especially among the drunks?'

'I've experienced plenty of sudden deaths,' said Jensen.

The man laughed.

'There, you see,' he said. 'I don't need to explain.'

'No,' said Jensen. 'What was it you found unbearable?'

'The hypocrisy, of course. The duplicity. The cowardice. The ruthless profiting from it all. Do you know what alcohol costs here?'

'Yes.'

'They impose several thousand per cent tax. That's an old right-wing idea, dictated by stupidity and greed in equal measure. It's proposed as one among other measures for combating abuse. The dearer the price of the alcohol, the fewer the cases of drunkenness. A completely absurd thesis, but even the teetotal brigade within the so-called labour movement were tricked into accepting it. Or rather, perhaps, pretended they believed in it. It makes no odds, because they're all as bad as each other; extortion or criminal stupidity, it's all the same.'

'Go on.'

'With what? Can't you see the bigger picture? We know people have to have alcohol, some so they can bear to carry on living, some for the courage to do away with themselves. So the prices are hiked, and the state's put to work, first criminalising the use of alcohol and calling it abuse, and then poisoning the drink with substances that supposedly wean them off it, which in turn generate deeper depression and lead to even more suicides.'

'You ought to watch your tongue.'

'Why ought I? Are you thinking of pulling it out?'

Jensen had made the comment out of sheer routine and force of habit. He felt a vague sense of surprise and stroked the tip of his nose.

'We've got the highest suicide rate in the whole world, and rates of drunkenness as high as in the most perfidious capitalist dictatorships. We've also got the lowest birth rate. Since the regime finds this worrying and is also a little bit ashamed of its own impotence, they try to lie it all away.'

'Well,' said Jensen, 'what actually happened in September?'

'Just a minute, let me finish my argument. So what do they do then? Well, they punish the individual for being forced by them to become an alcoholic, just as they punish people they've forced to live in substandard housing. They also punish the workers because they haven't bothered to teach them that work can be a meaningful end in itself. They even persuade us to pollute the very air we have to live in. Whole classes of society have to endure this curious form of punishment. The only ones who can escape are the profiteers, who can afford to live abroad

or buy big houses in the forest or their own islands in the archi-
pelago. It all hangs together, emanates from the same evil root.
Now do you understand why I find my work unbearable?'

Jensen did not answer that question. He looked past the
man on the sofa and said:

'Was it that way of thinking you wanted to launch through
your demonstrations?'

'Among other things. But anyway, launch isn't the right word.
We weren't presenting anything new. We just wanted to remind
people about a phenomenon they already knew about deep
inside, though they'd done all they could to forget it.'

'What phenomenon?'

'The class struggle. Can I have something else to drink?'

Jensen took the plastic cup and filled it up again.

'Thank you. Can I ask you something?'

'What?'

'Do you drink alcohol yourself?'

'Yes,' said Jensen. 'Or I used to, anyway.'

'Every day?'

'Yes.'

'Why?'

'The same reason you take tablets. I was in pain.'

'Was that the real reason?'

Jensen looked at the man for a long time. Finally he said:

'If we can go back to what happened in September.'

'I can't explain it. Everything changed. And everybody.'

'How did you yourself change?'

'I didn't change. At any rate, I had no sense of doing so. It
was the world around me that changed. Do you think that
sounds strange?'

'Yes.'

'It was, very strange.'

'When did you first become aware of it?'

'The third Saturday in September. The twenty-first.'

'In what context?'

'We used to demonstrate on Saturdays.'

'I know.'

'For practical reasons. Most people were at home and off work then. This autumn we upped the tempo because of the election campaign. Not that we had much hope of success. I mean, the Accord's propaganda machine had been steam-rollering away all spring and summer. They had every conceivable resource, as usual. We had nothing at all. We weren't even thinking in terms of the election result, yet we still thought we knew . . .'

He gave a start, suddenly on the alert. His eyes darted to and fro.

'Nothing to worry about,' said Jensen. 'Just a drunk getting a bit carried away down in his cell. What did you think you knew?'

'That there was pause for thought at the highest levels. Voter turnout had been going down every time over a period of quite a few years. Rumour had it that it was starting to annoy the regime. In its supreme stupidity, it didn't understand why people weren't voting for its excellent system. I'm talking mainly about leading figures in the trade union movement and former members of the social democratic party. The capitalists, the ones really pulling the strings, knew better of course. At any rate, that was the reason why the election campaign was so intensive and waged on such a broad front.'

'And what did your lot do?'

'We thought we'd do what we could to annoy them even more. That was why we focused so much on the demonstrations. It didn't seem to help, though. People were as indifferent as ever. Until that day, the twenty-first of September.'

'Did you demonstrate that day?'

'Yes. We organised an anti-imperialism protest march. It was going to start in the suburbs as usual and move in towards the centre. And we were going to round off with a public meeting. They mostly followed the same pattern.'

Jensen nodded.

'I went out to the assembly point by taxi with two friends of mine. A printer and his wife. My best friends. They were the same age as me, and members of our society. We'd known each other for years. Worked together a lot.'

'Worked? On what?'

'We did a lot of the society's practical work. Printed leaflets, did poster designs. Made placards and banners. Lots of other stuff, too. We had a duplicating machine and produced a little news-sheet for distribution to members. Yeah, we'd known each other a long time and very well.'

'Did they have any children, those people?'

'No.'

'What was the woman's job?'

'She worked in an archive at the Ministry of Justice. Later it turned out that . . .'

'Yes?'

'No, nothing.'

'Are you married?'

'No. Why are you asking me this?'

'Routine,' said Jensen. 'Anyway, to get back to that Saturday.'

'Yes. So we went out to the assembly point, but for some reason we got held up and were late. I don't remember why. Does it matter?'

'No.'

'When we got there, they'd already moved off. We met them as we were coming off the motorway.'

The man fell silent and looked towards the window. Outside it was sleeting, and big wet flakes were sticking to the glass.

'It was a clear, very blustery day. I remember the wind tugging at the flags, and the people with the banners had a job to keep them up straight. As soon as we caught sight of it in the distance we remarked to each other how beautiful it was.'

'Beautiful?'

'Yes, with the red flags whipping in the wind. And our comrades struggling with the breeze to keep the placards and banners up.'

'How many marchers were there?'

'A couple of thousand or so. We rarely got more than that. Often not even that many. There were quite a few children as well. Those with small children usually brought them along to demonstrations.'

'Why?'

'Oh, various reasons.'

'Such as?'

'So the kids had the chance to learn something sensible from an early age. To show anybody watching that there were in fact people who had children and thought they were fun to be around. And not least because there wasn't anywhere else for them to go, of course. Daycare provision is virtually nonexistent in this country, and socialists don't tend to have domestic servants.'

'I understand.'

'Good. So we met the march just as we came off the motorway and even as we passed, we noticed something unusual was happening.'

'What?'

'There were groups of people at the sides of the road, arguing with the demonstrators. Some were shouting insults, others were throwing things – empty bottles and cans. In one place I saw some of them scuffling with a uniformed police constable.'

'Why?'

'The police were trying to stop them rushing out into the road and attacking the marchers. At that stage, the police must have had orders to make sure the demonstrators were left in peace. You ought to know that better than I do. Am I right?'

Jensen nodded.

'Yes, that's correct,' he said.

'Admittedly most of the people driving past or on the pavements seemed totally uninterested, but there were some counter-demonstrations as well.'

'And what did you do?'

'We got out of the taxi and joined the march.'

'And then?'

'It was the same the whole way along. Lots of people were standing along the pavements hurling abuse at us. Some threw eggs and tomatoes. My friend's wife got hit in the forehead by a tomato. It made her laugh. In a few places, people even threw small stones, and some tried to run up and grab our signs off us. The police stopped them. There were several cars following alongside the march the whole time, and the people in them were spitting and swearing at us.'

'What kind of people was it who attacked you?'

'I didn't get the impression that they were any particular kind. Most of them were well dressed and there were just as many elderly as middle-aged or younger ones. Men and women.'

'How did your group react to this?'

'We felt encouraged for the first time in ages.'

'Encouraged?'

'Yes, really. After all, our big problem was that nobody took any notice of us, not even the police. That was the first time we'd provoked any kind of counter-demonstration, or any reaction at all, come to that. We felt our message wasn't falling on deaf ears any more.'

'Was anyone hurt?'

'I don't think so. Nothing serious happened. The weapons employed were very largely verbal ones, you might say. People generally contented themselves with shouting and swearing and throwing bits of harmless rubbish. Tomatoes and empty beer cans can scarcely hurt anyone.'

'What happened next?'

'Our rally was the liveliest and rowdiest one I'd ever experienced. By that time, an awful lot more people had assembled in the opposing camp. They yelled and booed and barracked the speakers. But we had loudspeakers and loudhailers and were able to stick to the planned programme.'

'Did the opposition seem to be organised?'

'No. That was one thing we were pleased to notice. The troublemakers had no organisation at all, and that was one reason they couldn't really cause us any serious disruption, of course. It was as if each individual was acting spontaneously on their own. We talked about that afterwards, and my friend said he'd been struck by the fact that they were people of such widely differing ages. The obvious conclusion otherwise would have been that it was an organised counter-operation. That the regime had sent out patrols of some kind to undermine what we were doing, as part of its election propaganda. But it was clear that that wasn't the case.'

'How did the meeting end?'

'The usual way. We passed a resolution and then packed up our kit and everyone pushed off home.'

'And the next demonstration? What happened there?'

'Hang on a minute. There was one very peculiar incident, after the meeting. Something that seemed completely incomprehensible. I'll try to tell it as I remember it.'

Jensen regarded him expectantly.

'When the meeting broke up, I went off with my friend and his wife. We'd been planning to go to our society HQ and finish off some posters we'd started the night before. My friend had a red flag rolled up under his arm.'

The man on the sofa lapsed into silence and seemed to be collecting his thoughts. Jensen said nothing. Down in the cells, the solitary alcoholic gave a series of hoarse, hacking coughs.

'Our premises are in a basement over on the east side. To get there you have to take the ferry over the canal, unless you're going by car of course. Pedestrians aren't allowed through the tunnel or across the bridges, as you know. There weren't many people on the ferry, and nobody seemed at all bothered about us. We sat on our own, chatting about what had happened. We all thought the same thing, namely that we ought to be encouraged by it. We got off the ferry when it had docked and walked the rest of the way; our HQ isn't that far from the ferry station. On the way you go through a rather posh, upper-class district. You know that area between . . .'

'I know the area you mean.'

'We were walking three abreast along the pavement, not saying anything at that point. The street was empty except for two elderly people standing outside the entrance of one of the buildings. I assumed they lived there and were on their way in.

The man must have been around sixty-five or maybe nearer seventy, and the woman looked about the same age. They were both well dressed, typical old-school, upper-class, right-wing types. The man was wearing a grey felt hat, black overcoat and galoshes, and he had an umbrella with a crooked, silver handle. I naturally wouldn't have registered those details if it hadn't been for what happened next.' The man on the sofa fell silent again and shook his head.

'I still don't get it,' he said. 'It was utterly absurd.'

'Get to the point,' said Jensen.

'Just as we're passing, the man says, "The devil take you, you goddamned riff-raff." My friend, who's nearest to him, doesn't take it in immediately, or maybe he can't believe his ears. Anyway, he stops and says very politely, "Excuse me?" And the man stares at us and says, all high and shrill: "Bloody rabble, how dare you show your faces here?" None of us have seen this man before, or his wife for that matter, so my friend says: "I'm sorry, but do we know each other?" Then the man grabs his jacket and shouts: "Do you think I don't recognise you, you damn socialist bastards!" Then the old biddy – yes she really was an old biddy – starts screeching and yanking at the flag my friend's got under his arm. They're totally hysterical. The woman manages to grab the flag and hurls it to the ground and starts spitting and stamping on it. Then she whacks my friend's wife in the head with her handbag as hard as she can and bellows: "Communist whore!" They both seem completely off their heads. The man raises the umbrella as if it's a rifle with a bayonet and jabs the point in my friend's chest, several times with full force. My friend falls to his knees and the old biddy grabs him by the hair and tries to kick him. She's screaming at us the whole time, showering us with spit.'

The man on the sofa glanced quickly at Jensen and put his hand nervously to his chin.

'I just stood there, absolutely at a loss. I mean, they were old people and it didn't seem right to lunge out at them. In the end my friend's wife pushed them aside and grabbed the flag. Then we made off as fast as we could. The last thing we heard was the old man shouting after us.'

'What did he shout?'

'You don't deserve to live!'

There was a brief silence. The invalid said:

'I just didn't get it, and I still don't. But plenty of other incomprehensible things have happened since. The next day we did at least find out who those people were. A retired bank director and his wife. They had some aristocratic sounding name. As reactionary as hell, of course, but a very refined and courteous old gentleman. So they say.'

'When did you hold your next demonstration?'

'Exactly a week later. Everything was a good deal rowdier that time. There was a bigger crowd of onlookers, and they were a lot more aggressive than the previous week. The police had brought in reinforcements. We went through with them anyway, the march and the meeting. And we still thought it was to be viewed as a positive development. We even decided to demonstrate more often and on other days of the week, to confuse the opposition. There was a lot of inflammatory stuff about us in the press and on TV just then. But the mass media soon stopped their running commentary on events. Before long they weren't saying anything about them at all, even in news bulletins. And the papers didn't write a word. They were full of the usual old froth about film stars and famous people. While society was collapsing about their ears.'

'Collapsing?'

'Yes. Isn't that what's happened now?'

Jensen made no reply.

'Another disturbing thing came to light round about then.'

'What?'

'In our society we had several members who were doctors and medical students. Nobody had seen them since the beginning of September. One of them was the man who brought me here, your district doctor. They weren't at home and when we asked about them we got the same unvarying reply: that they'd gone off to attend a conference somewhere. My friend's wife, who worked at the Ministry of Justice, eventually heard they'd been arrested. We didn't know if it was true or not.'

Jensen said nothing.

'Presumably it was true, because practically every doctor with socialist sympathies had vanished. Rumours seeped out that they'd been taken into custody on the orders of the secret police.'

'There's no such thing as the secret police.'

'You're lying,' said the man on the sofa matter-of-factly. 'I know it exists. Or used to. The girl who worked at the Ministry was able to find out about it. They were called the security services, not the secret police, and they answered directly to the Justice Minister. Their main task seems to have been to keep a register of opinions, a catalogue of individuals with inconvenient political views.'

Jensen bit his lower lip. After a while he said:

'The Steel Spring. Is that phrase familiar to you?'

'The Steel Spring?'

'Yes.'

'No. I've never heard it before.'

The man grimaced and said:

'My legs are hurting again.'

'Do you want another tablet?'

'Yes.'

'One more thing. How did the next demonstration go?'

'Complete uproar. Chaos. Fights breaking out. Hordes of police, but they did the very minimum to protect us. Stones and empty bottles raining down on us. Lots of people wounded, on both sides. Thank God we had no children with us. The fascists, as we'd taken to calling them, were behaving as if they were out of their minds. It was the tenth of October, three weeks before the catastrophe.'

The man on the sofa tossed his head and gritted his teeth.

'It wasn't just the fascists who were crazy. Other people started going weird as well. My friend's wife, for example . . . can I have that tablet now?'

'In a minute. What was the matter with your friend's wife?'

'I'll tell you. Later. Now please let me have that tablet.'

Jensen put down his notebook. Then he shook a pill out of the tube and slid his hand under the back of the man's neck.

CHAPTER 20

Once the man on the sofa was asleep, Jensen went back to his office. He unlocked the filing cabinet where they kept the orders and rules of general conduct that came in from outside, places such as the police headquarters. He went back to the day when he had handed over command and got out the red folder with the list of the forty-three doctors who were to be arrested. Then sorted quickly through the files for the past three months, selected ten or so and put them on his desk. Sat down and began to study them. They were all red and had the same code name: Steel Spring. Two of them were further arrest lists and the rest were instructions about police conduct at demonstrations and the issue of firearms on such occasions. The first arrest list had a hundred and twenty-five names on it, the second four hundred and sixty. His stand-in had ticked some of the names, presumably those of people they had successfully detained. Other names had annotations like 'unavailable' or 'disappeared', and many simply had question marks beside them. The annotations were untidy and presumably done in great haste. As far as he could see, the police of the district had not been able to apprehend more than a fifth of them, and most of those were on the first list.

As with the original arrest order for the forty-three doctors, neither of these communications said who they were from, but on closer inspection he found they bore the seal of the Justice Minister. They also differed from the original list in that they had a short note appended, the same for both of them:

These people are security risks. They must be apprehended immediately and placed in detention. They will be collected later by security service officers.

The instructions for general police conduct in connection with street demonstrations also came direct from the Ministry, and when read in chronological order they indicated a clear trend. It was apparent that police efforts to stop street disturbances and riots had escalated markedly through the month of October.

The orders issued at the very end of September and start of October were pretty routine in nature and dealt mainly with general regulations for the maintenance of law and order and instructions for redirection of traffic. From the tenth of October onwards, the tone stiffened. All reference to protection of demonstrators disappeared and was replaced by talk of forceful intervention to prevent disturbances hostile to the state, and on the fifteenth there were directions for all police officers to be armed when on duty. Five days later, the limitations to police use of firearms then in force were lifted until further notice. This was justified with reference to the Riot Act.

The arrest lists had arrived in swift succession, one on the twenty-fourth and the other on the twenty-sixth of October.

There was only one red file of any later date in the archive. Its wording was somewhat cryptic:

In preparation for the anticipated action of the enemies of society on Saturday (2 November) routine surveillance of law and order will be reinforced by special army units. Further orders will be issued by word of mouth.

This order, too, bore the seal of the Justice Ministry. It was dated the thirty-first of October. According to the diary record, that was the day after large parts of the government and the top police commanders had left the country.

It was impossible to see which particular office within the Ministry had issued these orders, but they all bore the same code name: Steel Spring.

Steel Spring must therefore have something to do with the police.

Inspector Jensen once again consulted his stand-in's notes in the diary and compared them with what he had written in his own notebook.

A broad outline emerged.

From the twenty-first of September onwards, unrest of a political nature had occurred. It had grown more serious through October and culminated on the second of November.

After that day, calm had been restored and everything had returned to normal.

Eleven days later, the epidemic had broken out. Although all possible measures had been taken against it, it had reached such proportions that within two weeks, the authorities had lost control of the situation.

There was no verifiable link between these events.

Only four or five days previously, the medical authorities had stated that the epidemic was under control. But simultaneously, the state of emergency had been tightened and all lines of communication had been broken.

Police organisation had collapsed, and evidently all military structure, too.

These events did not seem to interrelate in any logical way.

Jensen turned over to another page of his notebook and read the last thing written there, a reminder to himself.

What was it about his friend's wife?

He wrote down two more questions.

What happened on the second of November?

What is the Steel Spring?

He pulled open a desk drawer and took out a transistor-type portable tape recorder.

The man in the room next door had woken up and was shifting about restlessly. Presumably he was trying to reach the cup of soda.

CHAPTER 21

'You were right,' said Jensen. 'There seems to have been a security service answerable directly to the Justice Minister. I wasn't aware of that.'

The man on the sofa laughed.

'That's great,' he said, 'having secret police who are so secret that not even the police know about them. Maybe the people who belonged to it didn't even know they worked there.'

'That seems unlikely.'

'Perhaps. Thanks to our special contact in the Ministry we were able to find out how the secret police came to be set up. More or less. Would you like me to tell you?'

'Not really. There are two other questions I want answers to.'

'Well I'll tell you anyway. Some years ago, they did away with the old security police. Do you remember?'

'Yes.'

'It had disgraced itself and become such a laughing stock here and abroad that it just couldn't be allowed to carry on. So it was abolished, its professionals were pensioned off and the secret registers were burned. It was officially left to the armed services to spy on each other and themselves.'

Jensen drummed his fingers on his notepad.

'Admittedly the military also kept on making grotesque blunders, like sending planes in over the ports of our socialist neighbours to see if there were any ships there, and trying to send old war criminals in disguise in as spies, putting them ashore from surfaced submarines. It didn't really matter that the planes were shot down and the infiltrators were caught before they even had time to ask the way to the nearest rocket base. It's pretty much taken for granted that reactionary military types will behave like lunatics, and anyway, you could always swear black was white and play the injured innocent for public opinion, which they did, at every opportunity. Besides, the military had already sold all the secrets worth selling, to the socialist states for money and to the capitalist countries for a pat on their star-studded shoulders. But the big question was: who was going to spy on ordinary people?'

Jensen looked uninterestedly out of the window. It had stopped snowing. Drizzle.

'So they made a virtue of necessity and abolished the ludicrous security police and burned its painstakingly but injudiciously compiled opinion register. But before they set fire to it and converted the archive space into a table tennis hall, they took photocopies of the documents and shipped all the material off to the Justice Ministry. And ever since, a few low-profile employees have been sitting there fiddling with their register and the budget they use for paying informers. It's as simple as that.'

'What was strange about your friend's wife?'

The man's expression changed. He looked at Jensen in obvious distress.

'She's dead.'

'Was that what you were referring to?'

'No. I only brought her up as an example of how people started to react abnormally. It wasn't just that lot throwing stones and bottles at us and driving their cars into pushchairs, or having hysterics like that reactionary bank director and his senile old bat of a wife, it was people one knew and thought one knew well. She . . . she suddenly started behaving differently.'

'In what way?'

'If you're going to understand this at all, you need to know what sort of person she was, and always had been. I knew her and her husband very well indeed, almost as well as I know myself.'

He frowned.

'She was a calm, sensible girl. Seemed a bit shy, but that was because she wasn't a spontaneous person at all. She always considered matters very carefully before she said or did anything, and she was a huge asset to us in the society. Thanks to her ability to keep a cool head, for example, she was able to hang on to that job at the Justice Ministry. She reckoned we'd be able to make good use of it at some stage.'

'Get to the point.'

'If you don't let me explain the background there'll be no point to get to.'

'Go on, then.'

'Like most of our generation, she was physically and mentally damaged by her environment.'

'In what respect?'

'Emotionally. It's a widespread phenomenon here, and when it occurs in someone whose character is fundamentally lacking in emotion, the result is obvious.'

'Namely?'

'Namely complete absence of sensuality. Zero interest in sex. Why do you think the curve of the birth rate graph looks the way it does in this country?'

'But she was married, after all.'

'That was just for practical reasons.'

Jensen sat in silence.

'Well anyway, that's the way she was. But some time in September or early October, she started to change.'

'In what way?'

'She got more worked up, more spontaneous. Seemed very nervy.'

'Was that all?'

'No. One day in the middle of October we were all hard at work at our club premises. I remember it was after the big affray on the tenth, because we were talking about what had happened then. We were weighing up whether to stop the demonstrations for the time being.'

'Why?'

'Several people had almost lost their lives that last time. Lots had got hurt. Everybody there had been scared by the violence and the police passivity. In fact we only ever had one more demonstration.'

He stopped, staring hollow-eyed at Jensen, and said under his breath:

'The second of November.'

'We'll come back to that. What happened that day in your club premises?'

'She and I were busy with the duplicating machine; my friend was mending banners and flags that had got ripped on the last march. We were running out of paper and he went out to get some more. We knew it would take him about twenty minutes.'

'Go on.'

'As soon as he left, she went into the other room. I didn't really think much about it. She was back almost straight away,

and came right up close to me. I didn't look up until she took
my arm. She'd taken off all her clothes. She was standing there
stark naked.'

'I see. And then?'

'She stared at me and I stared back. Then she said: "Fuck
me. Now. This instant." She wanted us to have sex.'

'Clearly. Was that all?'

'What more do you expect me to tell you? What she looked
like?'

'For example.'

'She had this really odd look in her eyes. Other than that
there was nothing remarkable. I'd seen her naked before. In
other circumstances, of course.'

'Such as?'

'Well, in the sauna. When we went swimming. Occasionally
when a number of us were sharing a room at a summer camp.
We weren't particularly prudish in our circles. She was a normal
girl with little round breasts, small, pale-brown nipples and
fairly broad hips. Black hair on her cunt.'

'Mind your language.'

'Genitals then, if you prefer. That was the other strange
thing, incidentally. Her genitals. They looked twice their usual
size, open, wet, it was running down her thighs. She was
standing with her feet wide apart.'

'What did you do?'

'I told her to get dressed, of course. But I had to say it five
times and even then she only put her shirt on. I got so tired
of her that I left before her husband came back.'

'Was that all?'

'Yes. And quite enough, too, as far as I'm concerned. Her
behaviour was completely absurd.'

'Perhaps not as strange as you think.'

'What do you mean by that?'

Jensen did not reply. Instead he said:

'What happened next?'

'To her?'

'No, in general.'

'Things got worse and worse. People were incredibly worked up. When we stopped holding our public meetings, they transferred their attentions to the embassies of the socialist countries. Mobs stormed one embassy and set fire to it. The police hardly bothered to intervene at all, even though they had guns by then. In the course of a few days, about ten residences and consulates closed and the staff were sent home.'

'And what did you do?'

'Nothing. Decided to wait and see. Then out of the blue came the announcement that the elections had been put off. That was on the twenty-first of October, less than a week before election day.'

'How was the announcement made?'

'In the papers and on TV and radio. A member of the government spoke. The Minister for Ecclesiastic Affairs, I think. He said very briefly that the elections had been cancelled until further notice and that people should revert to orderly behaviour. He urged everyone to stay calm. And at just the same time . . .'

'Yes?'

'At just the same time, all that official baiting of us socialists stopped. Nobody said or wrote anything about any event, past or present. It was as if it was all over. In actual fact it had only just started.'

'What happened on the second of November?'

'Something unimaginable.'

The man suddenly clapped his hands over his eyes. It was a few minutes before he could go on.

'It was announced on the Monday that the elections were being postponed. On the Saturday of that week, the police started detaining people. Lots of card-carrying socialists and their sympathisers were arrested and taken away. Some escaped. Two days later there was a new wave of arrests. That time we were better prepared and the police didn't catch as many. Lots left the city. We three stayed on. We had a room in the basement for emergencies that not many people knew about, where we were safe even if the police raided the society premises. The next day there was a complete about-face. That minister appeared on TV and radio again and said there'd been a series of errors of judge ment. He said the police had exceeded their legal powers and that the general public had misconstrued the situation.'

'What else did he say?'

'That the arrests were illegal and that everyone detained on political grounds would be released immediately. He stressed that he knew both the police's and the public's actions had been motivated by righteous national indignation, but that the methods used could not be tolerated.'

'Well?'

'That all sounded very fishy, but the fact is, all those arrested by the police were released the same day. Friends of ours told us they'd all been shoved into enormous basement rooms in the new and as yet unfinished central detox unit. They'd been pretty much beaten up by the police and guards, and then suddenly they'd been let out.'

The man still had his hands over his eyes. He spoke in a lifeless monotone.

'The next day there were more government bulletins. This time there was no actual spokesperson. The announcements basically said that the country had a democratic constitution and that everyone had the right to express their political ideology without fear of reprisals. They said the election would be held in fourteen days' time and that, as part of the final campaign phase, the Accord regime urged all socialists to take part in a mass meeting that Saturday, that is, the second of November. Military units would be called in to support the police in maintaining law and order. It was guaranteed that there would be no risk to life or limb. All socialist and radical left-wing organisations and societies were invited in writing. The venue named on the invitations was the city's biggest sports stadium. Representatives of the government and all other interested groups of citizens would take part in a major political debate there. The boulevard that led to the stadium was assigned to the socialists as the approach route for their demonstration and march. The police and military would close it to all other traffic.'

Jensen heard something and tried to interrupt to comment on it, but the man did not seem to notice.

'By the Thursday evening, army units with tanks and helicopters were showing up in the city. Virtually all the socialist societies had accepted the terms of the meeting. We were working hard on our preparations, like everyone else. Some of our comrades from the rest of the country travelled in to take part. On the Friday everything was completely calm. That night we slept for just a few hours on mattresses in our club premises, me and my friend, his wife and a few others. She'd been getting weirder and weirder. I hadn't been asleep for more than an hour when I was woken by . . .'

Jensen was listening to the sound of an approaching motor engine. Even before the vehicle thundered through the arch, he knew it was the jeep. The man on the sofa seemed oblivious.

'It doesn't matter, anyway. The demonstrators began to assemble for the march around ten in the morning, and we set off down the avenue at the appointed time, on the dot of eleven. We had at least ten times as many marchers as on any previous rally, but then it was the first time all the societies and organisations were taking part. The pavements were packed with people, but nobody was booing or jeering. Between the onlookers and the march there were lines of soldiers and uniformed police in close formation. The only vehicles on the street were police cars and the military armoured cars. The marchers moved slowly forward. Some started singing. Otherwise it was quiet. It was a cold, grey day with a light drizzle. And then suddenly, when we were about halfway, they threw themselves at us.'

'Who did?'

'All of them. Soldiers and police and onlookers. They howled like wild animals and started shooting. For the first few seconds there was utter chaos. I thought they were shooting in the air to disperse the marchers or scare us. But it only took a moment for me to realise they were shooting to kill and we'd walked into a gigantic trap that the panicking government had set so it could get rid of us. There were people dying all around us. They were shot or had their heads smashed by rifle butts. Children were trampled to death. People who tried to run away stumbled in the pools of blood and were mown down by the police horses. It was total slaughter, inhuman chaos. The three of us kept close together. Somehow we managed to slip down a side street. As we were running we could hear the shooting and the cries for help behind us. When I glanced back over my shoulder I saw a helicopter come in low over the roofs. They were firing from it with a machine gun. We hid under a viaduct until it got dark. Then we sneaked back to our basement. The whole time there were police cars and ambulances wailing along the streets. The hideaway in the basement was our only chance. We stayed there. That was what happened on the second of November. The biggest massacre in world history. You asked me, and now I've told you.'

'And then?'

'We just stayed there. I don't know how many days. Then my friend's wife got sick. She was delirious and said she was seeing everything through a red fog. She felt as if she was suffocating and kept trying to throw off her clothes. As she got worse and worse we realised she had to go to hospital. We drew lots for who was to help her get there, and it was me. We both helped her up to the street and then I carried her to the nearest emergency alarm point. It turned out to be evening. Down in the cellar we couldn't tell if it was day or night. It took a long time for the ambulance to come. The driver didn't want to take her. He said she had an infectious illness and would probably die. He told me to put her in the ambulance and come with her because I was doubtless infected, too, and had to be quarantined.'

The man still had his hands over his eyes and was talking in the same monotone as before.

'He was right, in that she died in the ambulance. When we got to the main hospital, they told him to take the body to the central detox unit. I, on the other hand, was taken in and put on a trolley in a corridor. They gave me some sort of injection that put me to sleep. When I woke up, two men in white coats were pushing the trolley along an endless, all-white underground corridor. One of them was very tall, the other very short. The tall one took huge strides. The little one had to run. I got the impression they were pushing the trolley very fast. They had a muttered conversation as they went along, and I could only make out the odd term, none of which made any sense. Once I saw their eyes, I realised they were insane.'

'One moment,' said Jensen.

'They must have given me another injection. The next time I woke up I was lying on a blanket on the floor in a big ward. I had no legs. The whole ward was crammed with cripples like me. Some of them looked like monsters. Lots were dead. Those who were alive were whimpering and groaning. There was an unspeakable stench in the room. I heard someone say: "Hey, I know this one." I saw a red-haired man bending over me. I knew who he was. He was a police doctor. Then I don't remember anything until I woke up here and saw you.'

The voice ceased abruptly. Its owner lay still with his hands covering his eyes.

Jensen turned his head and saw the red-haired police doctor standing in the doorway with his right shoulder leaning on the doorpost.

'Is this true?'

The doctor raised a warning index finger, took out a needle and a plastic phial, slotted them together and went quickly over to the sofa.

Jensen looked on in silence as the red-headed man injected the contents of the phial. The man on the sofa immediately relaxed and went limp.

The doctor arranged the blankets and then turned to Jensen.

'What did you say?'
'I asked if that was true or untrue.'
'Well,' said the doctor. 'Yes and no.'
'Which means what?'
'That everything he told you did happen, but that he's misinterpreting some of the facts.'

CHAPTER 22

Inspector Jensen sat at his desk in his office. He had just switched off the tape recorder. The red-haired police doctor was standing over by the window, looking out at the slushy snow.

'True or untrue?'

'True, but wrongly interpreted in parts.'

'How much of it has he got wrong?'

'A fair bit. Some things you'll have realised yourself, of course, on the basis of what you already know.'

'Yes.'

'You understand what the girl's problem was, for example.'

'Yes. She'd fallen victim to the epidemic.'

'The illness. And since he doesn't know that her reactions were symptoms of that illness, he finds them incomprehensible.'

'Yes.'

'So the interesting thing isn't her behaviour in itself, or the fact that she died in the same way as the woman down in the cells. The essential question is how she got the illness.'

'And can you answer that question?' said Jensen.

'No. Unfortunately. Not yet. Did you find out what that name meant? The Steel Spring?'

'No.'

'That's another of the questions remaining to be answered.'

The police doctor turned round.

'Analogous to the story about the woman, there's another detail I can correct. That's to say, what happened in practice during the massacre of the second of November. I've got a pretty clear picture of what happened.'

'Is the witness's account inaccurate?'

'No. He told you exactly what he saw and heard. But the conclusions he draws aren't correct.'

'Aren't they?'

'No. No. He perceived it all as an ambush and organised human slaughter. A death trap that he and two others had just happened to slink out of.'

'Wasn't it?'

'Yes, from his perspective. But that's inevitably subjective. In actual fact there were a great many demonstrators on the march sensible and quick-witted enough to get themselves to safety. And most of those didn't hide away in basements, cowering there until the police patrols tracked them down. No, they got away from here as fast as they could, to instigate countermeasures.'

'Away from here?'

'Yes, out in the country. In the forest.'

'Like you.'

'Like me. What's more, the attack wasn't anything like as well planned and executed as he thought it was. As far as we've been able to reconstruct the sequence of events, the police, military and groups of civilians attacked in a totally disorganised fashion. In their eagerness to get at the demonstrators, the police and soldiers were shooting each other and bystanders who weren't even involved. The automatic fire from the helicopters, for example, was completely indiscriminate and didn't have that much impact on our people, since the marchers had already scattered by then and were running off in different directions. Admittedly a lot of people were killed in all the confusion, but not as many as he thinks. And the deaths were more or less equally divided between the demonstrators, their attackers, and the mass of still indifferent people who unwittingly made up the third party. That's not to say I'm claiming the massacre wasn't planned. I'm sure it was.'

'But hardly by the government,' said Jensen.

'Ah, you've realised that much.'

'But it was planned, nonetheless. By whom?'

'I should think that's one of the questions the people who sent you here are rather desperate to have answered.'

Silence descended on the room. The doctor looked out of the window again. He didn't move a muscle, and seemed to be waiting for something he knew would be happening very soon.

'You seem calm,' said Jensen.

'Yes, there's no great hurry any more. The damage is already done, so to speak.'

He checked the time.

'Perhaps I ought to check the contact,' he muttered to himself.

He turned to Jensen and said:

'Come with me.'

They went to the radio control room. The police doctor connected up the receiving equipment and spent some time adjusting switches and dials. After a while he said:

'Evidently it's not quite time yet.'

'What are you doing?'

The man didn't reply. Instead he tuned in to another

wavelength. A few seconds later the familiar, indolent female voice could be heard.

'Come in vehicle fifty. Vehicle fifty, do you read me? Calling all vehicles, do you read me?' Her next comment appeared to be to someone beside her.

'They're not answering any more.'

'No. And they never will,' muttered the police doctor.

He turned off the switch.

'Better save the batteries,' he said. They left the radio control room. The invalid on the sofa was still unconscious.

When they got to his office, Jensen said:

'I'm going to ask you to answer a few questions.'

'No point,' said the police doctor, taking a seat in the visitor's chair.

'I shall ask anyway. People generally answer when I ask.'

'You misunderstand me. I mean there's no point as long as neither of us knows the answer to the crucial question. What's the Steel Spring?'

He stopped speaking and looked pensively at Jensen.

'I know someone who can tell you all you need to know.'

'Who?'

'The one who sent you here.'

'His Excellency?'

'No, he's a mere figurehead, for use on the election posters.'

'The minister?'

'Just so. He knows a good deal we don't. On the other hand, we know a thing or two that he's no idea about.'

He reflected a while longer. Finally he asked:

'Do you think you could trick him into coming here?'

'It would be hard.'

'There is another way.'

'Which is?'

'Force,' the red-haired man said tersely.

He stood up and walked briskly back to the radio control room. Jensen did not follow him.

CHAPTER 23

'I don't like you, Jensen,' said the police doctor. Inspector Jensen did not respond.

'Nothing personal. I don't like you because you're a policeman.'

They were next to each other in the front seats of the patrol car. Jensen had the sirens on and was driving very fast through the deserted business district of the city centre.

'You'll be able to go at this speed all the way,' said the police doctor. 'All the roadblocks have been dismantled now. Think you can get to the airport in ninety minutes?'

'Yes.'

'Then we ought to get there just about the time our friend's plane lands.'

'Are you sure he's coming?'

'Yes.'

'How did you manage that?'

'Easy. He was as pleased as he was surprised to see a fighter plane from his own bloody air force landing at the airport. And when he heard you were on board, he was even happier. So then the guys heaved him into the cabin and took off again. I'm sure that was the method they used to recommend for getting a woman you wanted, back in the old days. Persuasion, cunning and – as a last resort – force. A sort of escalation.'

Jensen passed the Royal Palace on one side and the Ministry

of Communication on the other. He drove by the coalition parties' central offices, and the Ministry of the Interior.

'All the answers are in there,' said the man with the red hair. 'But it's quicker this way.'

The vast buildings looked grotesque and oversized in the cold, grey afternoon light. Jensen drove down into the tunnel leading south.

'The police do have to exist, of course, but your form of police has always been a willing tool of capitalism and the plutocratic ruling classes. The police are too indoctrinated by those ideas to be open to reform. It's the same with the military. Even a socialist society needs police and armed forces, however. Socialist police and socialist armed forces, to be more precise. And that's why the old organisations need to be eradicated and replaced with new ones. So that's why I don't like you. On principle.'

He sat in silence for a while. Jensen said nothing.

'Once the reactionary forms of the police and military stop functioning for some reason, something happens which is known in the jargon as a revolutionary situation. Somebody has now been kind enough to wipe out the police and the military. We assume it happened unintentionally, and the forms taken by the process were disgusting. Not even the minority among us that went on most eagerly and rabidly about creating a revolutionary situation can be feeling particularly satisfied or delighted.'

Without warning, he clapped Jensen on the shoulder.

'You're on your own now, Jensen. Has it sunk in? There's only you left.'

'Yes.'

'This is presumably your last big moment. I don't want to

overshadow it. Is there anything I know that you haven't worked out yet?'

Jensen said nothing.

'Ask away. I can at least confirm a few of your assumptions.'

'Assumptions?'

'Conclusions, then.'

'About this illness,' said Jensen.

'Yes?'

'It's fatal?'

'Yes, invariably.'

'But there is a way of prolonging the patients' lives?'

'Yes.'

'Transfusions?'

'Yes.'

'How long?'

'That's not entirely clear. But it can't delay the inevitable for very long.'

'Have you been able to chart the course of the illness? Medically?'

'Yes. Essentially. It goes through a series of stages.'

'What stages?'

'The very first symptom is the loss of all inhibition. It affects the central and sympathetic nervous systems of the brain. A centrally-operating nervous system, if you will.'

'Hence the increased sexual activity?'

'Yes. It presumably owes more to the loss of inhibition than to the stimulation of the nervous system. And since people have been schooled by their environment and upbringing to dam up their emotions, the effect is all the more spectacular. Did you get a chance to read those confidential research findings on sexual behaviour that were circulated a few years back?'

'No.'

'They were extremely depressing. Frequency of sexual inter-course among people of active ages was once a month. Only ten per cent of all adult women had ever had an orgasm.'

He sat for a moment saying nothing.

'The project was set up because of concerns about the falling birth rate. They were apparently satisfied with the result to the extent that it gave a plausible explanation of why the birth rate was falling. Naturally, no one in a position of responsibility thought to ask why people weren't having intercourse and didn't want children. And those who did were advised to hold their tongues.'

Jensen looked impassively out of the window. He had switched on the headlights and their beams dissolved into the distance in the emptiness of the tunnel.

'And what's the next stage?' he asked.

'More psychosis. Normally repressed aggression is let loose, you hit anyone you feel like hitting, kill anyone you feel like killing. Your judgement becomes increasingly impaired. You resort to more and more radical solutions. Say you're a table tennis player: you might well think the best option was to kill your opponent, to take one very simplified example.'

'And then the physical symptoms make themselves felt?'

'No. We think we've worked out that the next stage is a sort of mental rebalancing, a return to normal. The person feels well and behaves as he used to before they got ill. He remembers what's happened but feels no anxiety about what he may have done in his aggressive period, and doesn't feel any responsibility for what he did, either. In popular terms we might say that there's a blank, but that this blank is part of the overall picture of the illness.'

'How long do they remain in that state?'

'A week. Maybe two. Or something in between.'

'And then?'

'In the final phase, everything goes very fast. The first symptom is exhaustion. Then come delirium, nausea and, a little later, a persistent headache. The person loses all sense of will and becomes entirely apathetic. Sees everything as if through a pulsating red mist. At the end there's a feeling of suffocation and intense claustrophobia. A short period of unconsciousness, immediately followed by death.'

'Why?'

'What happens medically speaking is a rapid proliferation of white blood corpuscles, while the red ones disappear. You could see it as a kind of free-floating tumour. The pathology is similar to what we find in leukaemia, but compressed into a much shorter time frame.'

'And it's incurable from the outset?'

'As far as I can see. I'm not aware of any effective treatment. Which naturally doesn't preclude there being some way of halting the course of the disease at an early stage.'

Jensen drove out of the tunnel. The industrial area was still deserted, but there were lorries and jeeps parked at both sides of the road. There were groups of armed men and women standing round the vehicles. Most of them were wearing denim overalls or green boiler suits. The debris from the roadblocks had been thrown down the gravel embankments.

'Your people?' asked Jensen without taking his eyes from the road.

The police doctor nodded.

'We'll meet a lot of oncoming traffic,' he said. 'But it should be a clear run in the direction we're going. Feel free to step on it.'

'Am I right in thinking the illness has one more stage?' said Jensen. 'After the patient has nominally died.'

'Yes. But I've got to be more hypothetical on that point. The moment of actual, physical death can be postponed with the help of blood transfusions. They keep the patient not only alive but also in good physical condition. For a time, as I said.'

'Go on,' said Jensen.

'But it doesn't stop the illness moving rapidly into its next phase, the stage after death as you so aptly put it.'

He stopped. Jensen said nothing more, but concentrated on the driving. At regular intervals they met columns of lorries on their way into the city. Green-boiler-suited men and women sat closely packed in the backs of the lorries. They were all armed.

'Where did you get the outfits?'

'Abroad. A long time ago.'

Five kilometres further on, Jensen said:

'I assume all the cases of this illness started at virtually the same time?'

'Yes.'

'And that the infection or trigger was distributed eleven or twelve weeks before death?'

'Yes,' said the police doctor.

A few minutes later he added:

'So that doesn't leave us much to choose from, does it?'

'No,' said Inspector Jensen.

CHAPTER 24

'Why did they amputate his legs?'

'Because they believed their own assertions,' said the red-haired man.

'Is that a reasonable explanation?'

'Yes. They were basing their calculation on three mistaken hypotheses. Firstly that a vast number of people, including themselves, were suffering from an illness. Secondly that this supposed illness was infectious. And thirdly that it could be cured.

'They kept themselves alive with blood transfusions but knew it was only giving them temporary respite. So they tried out other forms of treatment. They knew the man who brought the woman to the hospital had been in close contact with her, and assumed he was infected.'

'Were they trying to cure him?'

'Yes. Or rather, they used him. Carried out some kind of treatment. He became part of a series of experiments.'

'They meant no harm?'

'Just so. They meant no harm. You're very precise, Jensen.'

The police doctor regarded Jensen through bloodshot eyes. Fished a cigar stub from the breast pocket of his boiler suit.

'Exemplary in your precision,' he said. 'I think everything that happened was done without meaning harm. That's the philosophy of the Accord: that no one is to have evil thoughts or malicious intent. No one's to be worried or distressed or want to hurt anybody or anything. It's a doctrine that's been hammered into people's consciousness for decades. Why should doctors be an exception?'

Jensen did not reply.

'But they overlooked the fact that if you deny life's negative sides, then all the positive things start to feel abstract and divorced from reality, too.'

The police doctor lit his cigar stub, chewed on it and puffed out a cloud of smoke.

'Because there are positive sides even to Accord society, when all's said and done. But you couldn't see them. Could you, Jensen?'

Jensen remained tight-lipped.

'Three months ago when you were coming along this very road, were you curious about what dying would feel like?'

'Not particularly.'

'Did you wonder whether anybody would miss you?'

'Was the amputation part of the treatment?' said Jensen.

'The aftercare,' the doctor said drily. 'First he was given some kind of prophylactic treatment. They injected mustard gas or something similar.'

'Mustard gas?'

'Yes, it's not as crazy as it sounds. Or at any rate, there's some kind of rational medical reasoning in the background, even if it's rudimentary. When the treatment proved disastrous, they did the amputation, presumably to save his life. They were doctors after all, in spite of everything, and a doctor's job is to prolong other people's lives. Besides, they were trying to complete in less than a week a series of experiments that might normally be expected to take ten years or a lifetime.'

'So they're insane.'

'Utterly. The brain damage suffered in the first stage is irreparable. Even so, they acted with a certain logic.'

'They must have killed thousands of people.'

'Yes. Even more than that, probably. But only once stocks of blood plasma had been exhausted. They mounted raids to round up blood donors pretty much the same way you cast a net to catch fish.'

'What does it look like there? In the main hospital?'

'What do you think? A vast hospital, home to a thousand or maybe twice that many deranged doctors, all needing blood transfusions twice a day to stay alive. And working like . . . well, like crazy to find a way to cure an illness they're suffering from themselves and can't understand. Dug in behind fortifications of barbed wire and sandbags that they made the military put up before they let them die. What did those two in the ambulance say to you when they forced you off the road this morning? The very first thing?'

'Asked if I was sick or healthy.'

'Exactly. In their confusion they've got all the concepts muddled up. Like so many other mentally ill people, they see themselves as the healthy ones and all the others as sick.'

The doctor wound down the side window and let the cool breeze fan the interior of the car.

'If only people had listened,' he said absently.

'What have you done with them?'

'The ambulance crews?'

'Yes.'

'What you should have done with those two this morning. Killed them. We're going to storm the main hospital in an hour's time and kill the rest.'

He shrugged his shoulders and threw the chewed and disintegrating cigar stub out of the window.

'So it was your lot who took the children away?'

'Yes. It was all we could do at that point.'

Inspector Jensen swung up to the forecourt of the terminal building and parked the patrol car exactly where he had found it sixteen hours before.

'Do you know what, Jensen?' said the police doctor. 'There were actually people who missed you.'

'Like who, for example?'

'Like me.'

CHAPTER 25

'Have you been inside the main hospital precincts?' asked Jensen.

The red-haired doctor shook his head.

'Just outside,' he said. 'That's quite enough for now.'

'Where did you find the man who lost his legs?'

'At the central detox unit. They stopped guarding it yesterday. Not enough manpower, presumably.'

He paused.

'Maybe you can imagine what it looks like there. It was used as a prison at first. Then, when the main hospital and all the others were overwhelmed by the dead and dying, they started cremating the bodies there. A hygienic precaution, as they saw it. Soon everyone who clearly didn't have long to live was sent straight there. Except for certain privileged individuals, of course, who were part of the junta, as it were, and allowed to stay at the main hospital and be kept going with blood transfusions, while the darkness claimed their brains.'

'But that man wasn't even suffering from the complaint, was he?'

'Within a few days it became impossible to carry on burning the bodies, because those doing the cremating ran away or died themselves. But they carried on sending the bodies there, in military trucks. The transports were still going on, as late as yesterday.'

Jensen nodded.

'I saw a few of them,' he said.

'Those you saw wouldn't in the main have been people who died of the complaint, but the blood donors they'd rounded up, and then killed either at the main hospital or one of the help stations. They were also taking all those deemed to be hopeless cases to the central detox unit. Patients who weren't even worth extracting blood from. The man without legs was one of those.'

'Why didn't people put up any resistance?' asked Jensen.

'Because they didn't listen to us,' said the doctor. 'Because they've all turned into sheep.'

'An over-simplification,' said Jensen.

The red-haired man shot him a look.

'Of course it's an over-simplification. Besides, a number of people did resist, lots of them hid away and others escaped in a variety of ways. And you must also remember that they had armed sanitation soldiers at their disposal. Trained military units that they kept alive for three reasons: to guard the hospital area, to block off the roads to the evacuated city centre, and to escort the transports of blood donors. But that's still not an adequate answer to your question.'

'What question?'

'Why people didn't put up more resistance. The primary reason is that a reactionary elite among the medically trained people in this country has spent years building up and maintaining an inflated, dishonest and artificial authority on the doctors' part, which they felt gave them the right to treat those seeking help any way they liked, and the opportunity to make scandalous profits from lucrative private practices, while officially devoting their time to their senior consultancies in the state hospital system.'

Jensen said nothing.

'This system hasn't just been accepted by the government, it's been actively encouraged. The doctors have been able to strut round among ordinary folk like richly rewarded gods wielding power over life and death. Officially they've been in charge of departments and whole sections of the state hospitals. But while sick people sit in crowded hospital waiting rooms for hours and even days on end to be treated in an offhand way by some medical student or underling, they devote hours to private patients who're willing to pay for medical care they may not even need.'

He turned his head and looked reflectively at Jensen.

'And that's how, for many people, doctors have become universally prevailing symbols of supremacy. Just as the government and the authorities have to an increasing extent become abstract, distant, incomprehensible powers, mercifully allowing their tablets of stone to descend on people like manna from heaven. Tablets inscribed with laws and edicts announcing that things are self-evident or meaningless, and ultimately stripping the individual of all spiritual and intellectual autonomy and making him doubt his own reason. There, that's your answer, I think. To why so few people offered resistance.'

They were standing beside each other in a room on the second floor of the terminal building. Out on the airfield there was significant activity. The last of the vehicles that had been used to block the runways were just being towed away. Several helicopters and small planes were being prepared for take-off.

There were groups of figures in green boiler suits standing about on the tarmac. Just below the window were two young women and a man. They were armed and had belts of cartridges slung over their shoulders. Jensen noted they were smoking and chatting. But there was no exuberance in their manner, and their faces were mournful and grave.

'So of course that eventually led to a lot of doctors, in fact most of the junior doctors and medical students, becoming socialists. Partly as a matter of conscience and social awareness, but naturally to a large extent because they were systematically pushed aside and excluded from more lucrative positions.'

The police doctor wiped the condensation from the window. Outside it was grey and misty, with snow in the air. It would soon be getting dark.

'The reactionary, more established part of the medical profession, who were in the overwhelming majority, viewed us with great disapproval and naturally didn't neglect to report their worrying observations to the government, which passed them on to the political police.'

'The security services.'

'Well, whatever you want to call them. Hence the wave of arrests just as you were leaving.'

'I know how you got away. But the others?'

'They were taken to the detox unit, where they were reasonably treated to start with. They weren't subjected to interrogation and there didn't seem to be any form of investigation in progress. The guards gradually got more brutal, and after that bloody Saturday, the second of November, they began executing the prisoners. Evidently on their own initiative, not on orders. Then my colleagues rioted en masse and staged a break-out. More than half of them got away while the place was in uproar. They headed straight out of the city and away from the surrounding area.'

It was starting to sleet again. The man with the red hair squinted towards the forest edge beyond the airfield.

'I'm assuming the national detoxification centre won't have a particularly good reputation among the public after this.'

'No, probably not.'

'I expect we'll have to blow the wretched place up and raze it to the ground with bulldozers. Then they can spread quicklime over the whole thing.'

'Doctors aren't exactly going to be popular either,' said Jensen.

The other man laughed, rather bitterly.

'Scarcely,' he said. 'Not after this reign of terror. Just think of the country's elite white coats, men and women, tearing around in howling ambulances. Like veritable werewolves, or vampires in fact. Bloodsuckers in the most literal sense of the word. It really was a week of unparalleled horror they inflicted on this city.'

'How many did they kill?'

'A fair number. But not as many as one might be tempted to think. They were only able to carry out their swoops on a relatively small number of residential districts. And even in those, they didn't catch everybody.'

'Why didn't you intervene sooner?'

'Our resources aren't that extensive. Even though we'd made various preparations over the years, it still took time to organise and assemble the scattered groups. What's more, we were psychologically unprepared. Who the hell would have thought the entire police force and military would self-destruct within a week?'

The electric lights flickered into life for a second and then went out again. A few moments later, they came back on.

'There we are,' said the police doctor. 'Things are starting to sort themselves out.'

He peered out at the inhospitable weather.

'Ah, here comes our guest.'

A delta-winged military plane had appeared above the trees. It landed on the far side of the airfield. The brake chute opened.

'Your last big interrogation, Jensen,' said the man with the red hair. 'Do you want me to stay to give evidence?'

'If you like,' said Inspector Jensen.

CHAPTER 26

The minister was escorted by a slim, dark-haired woman toting a sub-machine gun and wearing a red star just above the breast of her boiler suit. She looked about twenty-five. When she opened the door, the minister said:

'What are those flags on the roof?'

'Are you colour blind?' the girl responded.

She shoved him over the threshold.

'I'll be standing outside,' she said, and slammed the door shut.

The minister looked around him in confusion, but seemed pretty much as before, arrogant and supercilious.

He was still a young-looking forty-year-old with a slight squint in his blue eyes and an effeminate touch around his mouth. He was discreetly dressed in a grey worsted suit. Many people had found his appearance pleasing, but he hadn't made it on to the election posters, where the senior minister's greater weight and more earnest, everyday look had been considered a better symbol of security and prosperity.

The minister had used the social democrats' party apparatus as a springboard and risen rapidly in the Accord administration.

'I was kidnapped on foreign soi—'

He caught sight of Inspector Jensen and broke off abruptly.

'Jensen? Was it you who had me abducted like this? If so . . .'

'No,' said Jensen. 'It wasn't me. Please sit down.'

The minister sat down. He still looked perplexed, but perhaps also a little relieved. He apparently took Jensen's presence as an indication that nothing particularly serious had happened after all. Finding himself with an individual used to taking orders, who he could presumably boss about, seemed to boost his self-confidence.

Jensen had been standing behind the little desk when the man came into the room. Now he, too, sat down. Took out his notepad and pen. Regarded the visitor impassively.

The minister threw a look of irritation at the red-haired police doctor, who was standing over by the window, silent and still.

'Who's that?' he asked.

'My police doctor. From the Sixteenth District.'

'Ah, I see. Has the epidemic been contained?'

'Yes, it's over.'

'No further risk of infection?'

'No.'

The minister gave a sigh of relief.

'Thank goodness,' he said.

Then he recalled the assault he had recently suffered, and a menacing glint came into his china blue eyes.

'Who was responsible for my abduction?' he said. 'How could it happen?'

'Since the country you've come from doesn't officially exist for us, we don't have to stick too rigidly to protocol,' said Jensen.

His face was smooth and impassive.

The man eyed him suspiciously, but refrained from comment.

'When we last met, almost exactly twenty-four hours ago, I

took on the task of clarifying the situation here and investigating the circumstances that led to it.'

'Yes. But if the epidemic's over, there's nothing to investigate, is there? What's the meaning of that charade outside?'

Jensen flicked through his notebook, unconcerned.

'Who's the girl with the firearm? Presumably it's not loaded?'

'Unfortunately the investigation isn't yet complete,' said Jensen. 'I shall have to ask you to answer one question.'

'Me? Are you going to interrogate me?'

'Yes.'

'Have you gone mad, Jensen? If you've uncovered anything, then out with it, man. And after that, get me back to the Ministry as quickly as possible. In fact, give me your report in the car on the way.'

He got briskly to his feet.

'Is it true that the epidemic has been contained? That there's no risk of infection?'

'Yes.'

'Then stop beating about the bush and get yourself over here.'

'I think it would be unwise of you to try to leave this room, bearing in mi—'

'I don't know what you're talking about. Now get a move on.'

'Bearing in mind the risk to your security.'

'The police and army will no doubt see to that. Pass me the phone.'

'The phone isn't working. Even if it were, it wouldn't help you. The police force and the military system have been put out of action, at least temporarily.'

'Out of action? What the hell are you talking about?'

The minister gave Jensen a withering look.

'Sending a policeman,' he said to himself. 'I always said the man was an idiot.'

He gave a shrug of irritation.

'What could possibly have put the police and military out of action, as you say? War? Invasion?'

'The illness,' said Jensen.

'Rubbish,' said the minister. 'And anyway, the people are loyal. Blockhead.'

The police doctor had left his station by the window. He moved very softly in his rubber boots. With a couple of long strides he was half a metre behind the man in the elegant grey suit. He raised his right arm and struck him hard on the back of the neck with the side of his hand. The minister fell headlong to the floor.

'That's how loyal the people are,' the doctor said. 'Now get up and keep your mouth shut unless you're asked to speak.'

Jensen regarded him coolly, with a look of distaste.

'That,' he said, 'was entirely unnecessary. If there's any repetition I shall end the interrogation.'

CHAPTER 27

The minister sat in the chair opposite Jensen. His eyes shifted uneasily and he dabbed the blood from the corners of his mouth with a rolled, white silk handkerchief. The red-haired police doctor was back in his place by the window.

'A few brief facts,' said Jensen. 'To sketch in the background to the question I want you to answer.' The minister glanced surreptitiously at the window and nodded.

'Many thousands of people have died of the illness that struck some sections of the community. In point of fact, it's not correct to call it an epidemic, because the illness has proved not to be infectious.'

The man on the other side of the desk frowned deeply.

'The chaotic situation that has prevailed in the country and above all in the capital for a period has arisen in part because a large proportion of the staff in the organisations that preserve the fabric of society have fallen ill and died.'

The minister had finished wiping away the blood, and put his handkerchief away.

'The centre of power over the past week has been a group of doctors and other healthcare workers, who've barricaded themselves into the main hospital and the area round it. It turns out that virtually all these personnel are suffering from the aforementioned illness. While attempting to cure both themselves and others they have become mentally ill, as a result of brain damage caused in the initial stages of the illness. A week ago, when most normal social functions had become paralysed, this group declared a state of emergency.'

The minister stared at him and moistened his lips with the tip of his tongue.

'The method the group at the main hospital used to keep themselves alive depended on frequent blood transfusions. Once stocks of blood plasma were exhausted, they began press-ganging blood donors, who were taken to the main hospital at gunpoint and killed there. It's still not clear exactly how many. When the state of emergency was declared, the whole city centre was shut off, and the few people who lived there were evacuated. Shortly after that, a total curfew was imposed on the whole metropolitan area. The population has been terrorised and living in extreme fear.'

The man on the other side of the desk opened his mouth to say something, but Jensen immediately held up his right hand to stop him.

'One more thing,' he said. 'It was been ascertained that all those who succumbed to this disease fell ill simultaneously, and must all have been exposed to the infection or trigger at practically the same time. This would have been about three months ago, that's to say at the very end of August or very beginning of September.'

'It's not my fault,' said the minister.

'In the light of this background information, I want to ask you to answer the following question.'

The minister stared at him as if paralysed.

'What's Steel Spring?'

Silence descended on the room. Outside, it was dusk. Jensen could make out low voices and a motorised throb, presumably a helicopter landing. He looked at his watch and let the second hand tick once round the dial. And again. Then he raised his eyes and fixed them on the man in the grey suit.

'Whatever's happened, it's not my fault. Not our fault. If anything's happened, it's a pure accident.'

The man's voice was hoarse and hesitant.

'What's Steel Spring?' Jensen asked flatly.

'Can . . . can I have a drink?'

'No,' said the police doctor from his station at the window. 'The waterworks aren't back in action yet.'

'Please answer the question,' said Jensen.

'Steel Spring . . .'

'Yes.'

'It was the code name for an operation that was part of the coalition parties' election campaign.'

'Who had responsibility for this operation?'

'The campaign leadership.'

'Were you personally a member of that campaign leadership?'

'Yes.'

'What did this special operation aim to do?'

'Produce loyalty propaganda, intended to stimulate citizens' political interest in the run-up to the election.'

'What form did it take?'

The minister was starting to regain his composure. He looked at Jensen with something approaching his customary chilly arrogance.

'Now listen here, Jensen, what has this got to do with anything? If something's gone badly wrong, neither I personally, nor my party nor the Accord as a whole can be made scapegoats.'

'Stick to the facts.'

'With pleasure. I have nothing to hide. One fact, for example, is that a number of different bodies within society collaborated in the implementation of the campaign and were responsible for its overall shape and its various stages.'

'The security services, for example?'

The man stole another look at the area by the window. At length he said:

'The security services had very little to do with the operation as a whole. It's possible that they were involved in some small detail at the preparatory stage. In speaking about the security services, however, you must be aware that you are dealing with questions of an extremely confidential nature.'

'Not any more. You still haven't told me what form the operation took.'

'It was all very simple. They sent out a card with a statement of loyalty. You should have had one yourself.'

'Yes. That's right. A white card with a blue sticker.'

'Just so. Why are you asking lots of things you already know? Did you send the card in, by the way?'

'Yes.'

'Did you put on the sticker?'

'Yes,' said Jensen.

The minister looked quizzically at Jensen.

'What the hell is this actually all about?' he said.

'Who produced the cards?'

'Our largest private paper mill, newspaper and printing company.'

'And the envelope?'

'The same group of companies. You should know them. You of all people.'

'Who had responsibility for the stickers?'

'The National Bank's banknote printing works.'

'And who was responsible for the gum on them?'

The silence was even longer than the last. Every so often, there was a clatter from outside as the sub-machine gun knocked lightly against the wall. In the end, the police doctor straightened up. Jensen gave him a quick, expressionless look. Then he repeated the question.

'Who had responsibility for the stickers?'

'The Defence Research Institute,' the minister said quietly. He looked miserably in Jensen's direction.

'No,' said the doctor. 'No, it can't be possible.'

He stared at the minister as if stunned. Then he threw back his shoulders and went rapidly out of the room.

The minister gave Jensen a terrified look.

'No,' he said. 'For God's sake don't let him . . .'

Inspector Jensen did not move. Out in the corridor, the police doctor threw open the door to the toilet next to the office. Almost at once they heard him being sick.

The wall was thin and far from soundproof. The terminal building as a whole was a scandalous bit of jerry-building. It had been put up by a private entrepreneur when the current Education Minister had been serving on the building committee.

At the same instant, the water pipes started to gurgle.

CHAPTER 28

'Pardon me for interrupting,' said the police doctor, 'but I thought it was important to clarify the details. Partly because it saves time, partly because it seems to me the most honest way to do things.'

Jensen nodded.

'I understand,' he said.

The police doctor turned to the minister again, gave him a savage look and said:

'Have you got that?'

'As a professional politician I've had to learn to assess and evaluate situations.'

There was still an undertone of arrogance and pride in his voice.

'Maybe you're not a very quick learner. As far as I can see, you've completely misinterpreted everything since you arrived. Not least the situation in which you find yourself. So allow me to repeat what I just said. Your chances of getting out of here are extremely limited; in actual fact they are so tiny that it might be considered debatable whether you'll even make it out of this room. I was very close to laying hands on you myself a minute ago. And I can assure you there are a lot of people here with a good deal less patience than me.'

There was nothing self-controlled about the way the minister was looking at him.

'He's scared,' said Jensen unsympathetically. 'You've already given us proof of that and I don't see there's any point in labouring it. A witness in a mentally balanced state is in principle always preferable to one who's scared out of his wits and feeling physically and/or mentally threatened.'

'Standard police instructions,' the doctor said drily. 'But you're misinterpreting my motives. For me this is primarily a moral question, not a matter of convenience. Just as you like preserving your antique office equipment, so I like to stick to a few archaic ethical values. They both come in handy sometimes.'

Jensen refrained from answering.

'Have you finished your private chat?' asked the minister.

'Yes.'

'In that case let me inform you that I fully understand the implications of what you said. If I don't prove compliant on every point, you'll have me butchered. You may even do it personally.'

'That's about it,' said the doctor.

'For me, that's a very persuasive argument. What do you want to know?'

The police doctor said nothing further. He nodded and returned to his place by the window.

Jensen studied his notes. A minute or two went by, and then he said:

'You're claiming the agent was considered to be harmless?'

'Yes. Otherwise we naturally wouldn't have used it.'

'Who suggested using it?'

'It wasn't me.'

'Who?'

'That's a complicated question. It requires me to explain various things.'

Jensen gave the man about thirty seconds to muster his thoughts. Then he said:

'Go ahead.'

'The Defence Research Institute was a financially profitable company. Over the years, its scientists developed various very successful products, particularly in the biochemical field. These were produced under licence abroad, and provided a significant flow of foreign capital into our country, to the general good.'

'Were these products intended for military use?'

'Usually. Herbicides and defoliants, and humane bacteriological warfare agents.'

'Humane?'

'Yes, agents not aimed at direct human extermination, but designed to put enemy troops or recalcitrant groups temporarily out of action. Here in our country we had no use for such weapons of course, but in other parts of the globe they were very effective in the fight against world comm—'

He broke off and glanced over at the man by the window.

'Go on,' said Jensen.

'But there were certain disadvantages to bacteriological warfare, and some years ago it became obvious that in a wealthy world market there was a need for a biochemical weapon with the effect I mentioned. Rendering enemy forces temporarily harmless, making them incapable of defending themselves.'

'Yes?'

'In other countries there had already been some efforts in that direction, but the results were unsatisfactory. Admittedly they had developed a few trial products, but they all proved defective in some respect or other. What's more, some of them did considerable harm, since the secret of their existence got out to the public, who used them as narcotics. We even felt the effects here at one time. Psychedelic drugs that were smuggled in and abused by the depraved youth of the time. Do you remember?'

'I remember,' said Jensen.

'Anyway, a group at the Defence Research Institute started looking into the subject. A team of trained research scientists that had previously achieved profitable results in other areas. Their activities were shrouded in the greatest secrecy of course, which was a very natural condition insisted on by the foreign interests that had invested the capital.'

'Who had access to the results?'

'Apart from the clients, only one special committee within the government. Where appropriate, the security services and the top military leadership were also informed.'

'And were you yourself a member of this special committee?'

The minister hesitated.

'Yes,' he said finally. 'There would be no point denying it.'

'Go on.'

'As far as I understood it, this is what happened. What they were searching for was an agent with the capacity to render certain individuals within, for example, armies of hostile groups passive for a time. The research and development was taking a long time, our clients gradually lost patience and made repeated representations to the special committee through diplomatic channels. They demanded no less than to be shown the results that had been achieved to that point. This finally led the committee to demand the same of the research institute. About two years ago, the head of the research team sent the committee a memorandum.'

A loudspeaker began to boom somewhere in the building. The minister jumped.

'The radio,' said the police doctor tersely. 'A so-called historic moment.'

'What was in the memorandum?' asked Jensen.

'For a layman, what it had to say was not only incredibly complex but also very blunt. It said work was proceeding normally . . . but to cut a long story short, they had no results whatsoever to show as yet, that the costs had spiralled and budgets were overspent and that furthur grants would be needed if work was to carry on.'

'Was that all?'

'No. There was an appendix to the dossier.'

'Yes?'

'We read it more or less as an attempt at evasion. It said they had pursued their research on the basis of some kind of antithesis method, and sure enough they had come up with a number of by-products, among them a preparation that hadn't yet been fully tested. It was known by its code number and was considered promising. For us, on the other hand, it seemed anything but promising, since it was evidently the complete opposite of what the financial backers thought they had a right to expect.'

'Insofar as what?'

'The agent in question had been shown to stimulate the will and the urge to achieve targets. They thought they could develop it quite quickly for military use. Battle-weary soldiers could be made more aggressive, more eager to fight and mentally more consolidated. For now, there were various disquieting side effects to contend with. The agent brought with it a kind of hangover, similar to that seen in alcohol abuse. It also led to the abandonment of inhibitions, most obviously in respect of sexual behaviour. They were confident these side effects could be eradicated in the foreseeable future. The preparation was called D_5H.'

The man stopped. Appeared to be thinking. Then he said:

'That was the gist of it. We sent the dossier on to the clients, who replied at once that they could invest no more capital on such meagre results.'

'And what about D_5H?'

'On that point, their reply was wholly negative. They said they had more than enough alcoholics and troublemakers, not to mention drug abuse and promiscuity.'

'And what was the committee's reaction to that answer?'

'There was only one way it could react. The Defence Research Institute isn't some charitable employment scheme. We immediately cancelled the whole project and transferred the staff involved to more lucrative activities. We heard no more about it until a couple of months ago.'

He gave a dry, racking cough and put his hand over his mouth.

'Then the individual who had invented D_5H informed us that he had completed the research on his own initiative with the help of a female assistant, and that the preparation had now been through a full set of trials. He was given permission to appear before the committee in person, and came across to us as extremely enthusiastic.'

'What does D_5H stand for?'

'The letters are just the inventor's initials. The five was some kind of serial number, I suppose.'

'Carry on.'

'The agent was available in tablet form at that stage. According to its originator, it stimulated the will, and the drive to achieve goals, to an extraordinary extent, while arousing the subjects' interest in their surroundings and refining their thinking.'

'Refining their thinking?'

'In that it made it easier for them to express emotions they already had. For example: affection, determination to win, loyalty, love, always assuming these feelings were directed at specific individuals or concepts. One side effect remained. The agent was a sexual stimulant. But since it was also goal-orientated, it wouldn't necessarily lead to promiscuity, in fact just the opposite. This was what the inventor told us, anyway, and he was also kind enough to point out that our people, with their falling birth rate and extremely underdeveloped sexuality, had long been in need of serviceable aphrodisiacs.'

'Well he was right about that,' said the police doctor.

Jensen silenced him with a look and said:

'Well?'

'The man asked for permission to try D_5H on human subjects. First individuals, then trial groups.'

'And?'

'As far as we could see, there was no reason to turn down his request.'

'How did the trials go?'

'Very well indeed. The tablets were initially given to boxers who were expected to lose. They won. Then other individual sportsmen, and then a football team. With excellent results all the way. The agent took effect immediately and did everything its originator had promised. The next step was experiments on people engaged in political activities, in our youth organisations and so on. I tried it myself, when I was at a congress. The effect was as intended, and the tablets weren't habit-forming or addictive. One could observe an instant boost in energy levels, although unfortunately only a very temporary one. It was also observed that the sexually stimulating effect was more noticeable among women than men. But that seemed to be it. Although D_5H worked, we had difficulty seeing any way of putting it to practical use. Above all because its effect was so transitory. The inventor personally, and his institute, were informed of this. We were not of the view that the tablets should be manufactured in larger quantities or released as pharmaceutical products, since in the wrong hands they might have undesired consequences.'

'What happened after that?'

'The researcher and his assistant demanded immediate permission to carry on working. They hadn't given up their original idea that the agent, as with other biochemical weapons, could be distributed in a form that meant people were not aware of being exposed to the effects. Moreover, they thought they were at a stage which meant they could soon intensify the impact of D_5H so it would remain active for four to six weeks. We let them carry on working.'

He fell silent and tried to catch Jensen's eye. When this failed, he sighed and said:

'In the early summer of this year, the inventor informed us that D_5H was ready for use. He was called in front of the committee to explain in greater detail what this meant. He explained that he and his assistant had solved all the known problems. The effects of the agent had been extended to about six weeks, after which they disappeared. They had also managed to delay the onset of the effect, so it made itself felt only after two to three weeks. Finally, he had solved the distribution question and established what to use as a vehicle or base. In this he had gone back to various ideas and partial results from the original research project. The idea was quite simply to dissolve D_5H in glue that could then be used for the gumming of stamps or stickers. Need I say more?'

'Yes,' said Jensen.

'The inventor said the costs of production were exceedingly low. He could quickly produce quantities sufficient for the adhesive for many millions of stamps. It would cost no more than the gum normally used on postage stamps. Furthermore, he said, the whole batch fitted into a few glass jars, and the agent would prove invaluable in the event of people needing to steel themselves for a coming crisis. He said that in airtight containers, the agent could be stored for an indefinite period.'

The minister put his head in his hands.

'We commissioned him to make enough of the product for a normal stamp issue, and keep it at the ready. On the first of August, he told us he had completed the task according to our instructions. He was given a bonus. And there's not much more I can tell you about the institute's role in this affair.'

'That doesn't answer the question about Steel Spring,' said Jensen.

'Yes it does,' the man said bitterly. 'The campaign committee for Steel Spring came under a lot of pressure from certain elements within the coalition parties. At the previous election, voter turnout had sunk to below fifty per cent; in actual fact only forty-six and a half per cent of all those entitled to vote did so. The figures weren't released, but they couldn't be kept entirely secret from the public. Comprehensive opinion polling showed that the vast majority of people who didn't turn out to vote and stayed on their sofas were employees in the lower income groups. The party to which I originally belonged was the strongest element in the grand coalition on which the Accord was based. This socialist and . . .'

'Don't let me hear that word in your mouth,' the police doctor said fiercely.

'. . . and democratic party had taken their votes from precisely those low-income groups. The unfortunate way things had developed meant that some groups began to question whether our party – or to be more accurate our *former* party – was over-represented in the current administration.'

'So you could be said to have acted in your own interests,' said Jensen.

'Not at all. I and everyone else on the campaign committee were working entirely with the best interests of the people in view. We knew that the people were loyal and supported both the notion of accord and our welfare policies.'

'But fifty-three and a half per cent didn't bother to vote?'

'That doesn't mean they didn't wholeheartedly support the regime.'

'What does it mean, then?'

'That large sections of the people didn't consider it necessary to manifest their loyalty to the regime. The outstanding results of our practical policies and the high standard of living lulled them into a sense of security.'

'But wasn't that security one of the central pillars of the Accord?'

'They could at least fucking well drag themselves to the polling stations once every four years,' the minister exclaimed.

'So it annoyed you?'

'Yes. And what annoyed us even more was that irresponsible left-wing elements were disturbing the social order. They only made up five or six per cent of the whole population, but were constantly staging groundless demonstrations and protests. They opposed everything, from the way we packaged the fizzy drinks, which I can guarantee is the most profitable method in the world, to our foreign policy, despite the fact that it's kept us neutral for more than a century. Thanks to the fact that we don't get involved in matters that have nothing to do with us and are often happening in faraway parts of the globe.'

He was speaking in rapid gasps and had to stop to catch his breath.

'Ninety per cent of the population saw these irresponsible factions as just childish, ranting on about the third world and imperialism and international conscience. I've said the same things myself in every single election campaign, by the way. And carrying on their propaganda for a revolution that we achieved with a stroke of the pen years ago. But despite all that, people didn't bother to repudiate or condemn them. Instead they were allowed to attract the young, who knew no better than to believe puerile doctrines coined by simple-minded foreigners. They were even given the leeway to infiltrate one of society's most important groups of professionals.'

'Which one?'

'Not the police. The doctors. Lots of medical students were infected by their propaganda even before qualifying. The loyal section of the medical profession was extremely concerned. When we discovered that this subversion was going on without any reaction from the people, we realised something had to be done.'

'What?'

'Steel Spring. We launched Steel Spring. The big loyalty operation that would spur the people into action once and for all. And show how superfluous and irresponsible all criticism of the ideas of wealth and accord really was. We decided to go in hard with the campaign, using all the means at our disposal.'

'Was D_5H one of those means?'

'Yes.'

The reply came almost in a whisper, but the next minute the man raised his voice all the more.

'Why the hell do you think I'd be sitting here giving away state secrets otherwise?'

'Go on,' Jensen said tonelessly.

'The doctors among the campaign leadership recommended it,' the minister said resignedly. 'They had tested and analysed the preparation themselves. Like the inventor, they guaranteed it was harmless as long as it wasn't distributed to any close-knit group of unreasonable, incorrigible people. The decision to deploy D_5H was unanimous.'

'And how was it deployed?'

'We used it for the gum on the campaign sticker, of course. Can't you work anything out for yourself?'

Jensen said nothing.

'We decided that we'd test the first batch on various professions whose loyalty could be guaranteed.'

'Which ones?'

'The professional soldiers, the police, the loyal doctors, the electoral societies, the customs service, the loyal youth movements, and staff at the ministries. In order to assess the effect, we timed the period in which the agent would be effective to coincide with intensive propaganda against the antisocial elements.'

'What other steps were taken?'

'The chief medical officer demanded that all doctors and medical students recorded as antisocial elements in the secret service archives be arrested and held in isolation while the campaign was in progress.'

'Why?'

'It was felt that there was a risk of one or more of them getting their hands on a stray sticker. And then having sufficient scientific knowledge to be able to analyse the substance and cause a scandal. If the truth got out about D_5H, the second phase of the campaign could be jeopardised.'

'What second phase?'

'Distributing the preparation to all workers in the low-income bracket in the form of gummed discount vouchers, timed to take effect the week before the election. Conventional propaganda in the press and on radio and TV would culminate in the same period. Experience and test results from the first batch would underpin our plans for the big, crucial push.'

He paused briefly.

'According to our statistical calculations, that would produce ninety-five per cent voter turnout. More than ninety per cent of people would vote for the Accord. The opposition would be silenced for good.'

The minister gave Jensen an imploring look.

'You do see, don't you, that it was all done in the people's interests? That we meant no harm? That we had no evil intent?'

'Your calculations turned out to be wrong,' said Jensen.

'Yes. And now, with hindsight, it's not difficult to work out certain causes and effects. Five days after the declarations of loyalty were sent out, the man who had invented D_5H died of leukaemia. He was almost seventy, and we didn't find the news alarming.'

'You didn't?'

'No. We granted him the honour of a state funeral. I walked in the mourners' procession myself.'

'When did you realise what was going on?'

'Personally I didn't understand until today. Initially, everything looked very promising. But in the middle of October, we started losing control of the situation. People's reactions were far more violent than we'd expected. The campaign degenerated. Within a week, there were as many murders and manslaughters here in the city as over the whole preceding five-year period. It went so far that the chief of police ordered that violent crime wasn't even to be recorded. Then we found out the police and military weren't obeying orders. Or to be more precise, they weren't obeying our orders but taking their instructions directly from the Ministry of Justice. When we tried to get hold of the inventor's female assistant, it turned out she'd destroyed all the research notes and the entire stock of D$_5$H. Then she'd committed suicide. On the twenty-first of October we were forced to postpone the elections. I made the public announcement myself. Five days later we discovered that the guards had taken it upon themselves to execute the doctors in detention. By the thirtieth of October the situation was completely untenable; the Regent and virtually all the top civil servants discreetly went abroad or to their holiday homes in distant parts of the country. After the riots on the second of November, things were calm. I came back to the city two days later, along with a number of other government officials in positions of responsibility. We launched an investigation, but there wasn't time to complete it. The epidemic broke out. Obviously we didn't see the connection. You know the rest better than I do.'

'Didn't anyone in the government or the campaign leadership lick one of those prepared stickers?'

'Only the chief medical officer. In the interests of research.'

The minister gave Jensen a look of appeal and said:

'I mean, you don't send out requests for declarations of loyalty to yourself, do you?'

'No. That's right.'

'Nothing was done with evil intent. Not a single bad thought was thought.'

Inspector Jensen did not reply.

The car containing the minister and the armed guards drove away. They stood there in the circle of light outside the main entrance doors of the terminal building, a few metres from the telephone boxes. Jensen looked at his watch. Exactly twenty-four hours had elapsed since he had stood there the first time.

'What do you plan to do with him?'

'It's not up to me,' said the police doctor with a shrug of his shoulders.

'He can scarcely be convicted of any crime.'

'Capitalism's a crime in itself. But it's a paper tiger. If anyone drops a spanner in the works, it's got nothing to fall back on. People are indifferent to it. They know nothing and under-stand nothing beyond the narrow sector of their own training. And the alienation makes them incapable of establishing connections.'

'I saw a camel the other day,' said Jensen.

'Really?'

'Yes.'

The temperature had dropped a few degrees and it was snowing.

'We ought to try to find a cure for leukaemia,' said the doctor.

'And now you're going to socialise this society of ours?'

'You can bet your bloody life I am, Jensen. And it's not going to be easy. Plenty of bad thoughts are going to be thought.'